THE ELUSIVE MR. PERFECT

A MODERN COUPLE FINDS LOVE ALONG UNEXPECTED AVENUES

TAMELA HANCOCK MURRAY

THORNDIKE PRESS

An imprint of Thomson Gale, a part of The Thomson Corporation

THOMSON
™
GALE

Detroit • New York • San Francisco • New Haven, Conn. • Waterville, Maine • London

THOMSON

GALE

LIBRARY OF CONGRESS CATALOGING-IN-PUBLICATION DATA

Murray, Tamela Hancock.
  The elusive Mr. Perfect : a modern couple finds love along unexpected avenues / by Tamela Hancock Murray.
    p. cm. — (Virginia hearts ; #1)
    ISBN-13: 978-0-7862-9805-1 (alk. paper)
    ISBN-10: 0-7862-9805-7 (alk. paper)
    I. Title.
PS3563.U789E48 2007
813'.54—dc22   2007019787

Published in 2007 by arrangement with Barbour Publishing, Inc.

Printed in the United States of America on permanent paper
10 9 8 7 6 5 4 3 2 1

Dear Reader,

Thank you for choosing to spend time with the stories in *Virginia Hearts*. I am a native of Virginia, and the state is indeed close to my heart.

My family has lived in Virginia for many generations. I grew up in a close-knit, God-fearing family in the Piedmont region of Southern Virginia. I graduated from Lynchburg College with honors in journalism.

Now my home is in Northern Virginia with my wonderful husband of over twenty years and two lovely daughters. The elder attends Lynchburg College and is the fifth generation of my family to do so. Our younger daughter hopes to matriculate there as well.

Daddy says I'm a Yankee since I live north of the James River. As far as I'm concerned, I'm still a Virginian, even though life so close to Washington, D.C., moves at a faster pace than the speed my relatives in the country enjoy.

When you read these stories, I hope Virginia will come alive for you. In noting scenery, I recall times of enjoying the smell of falling leaves, the sight of crystalline blue skies, and the warmth of Virginia sunshine. When a restaurant is mentioned, sometimes I have dined there myself. Perhaps you might try some of these places when you visit Virginia. If you haven't already traveled to my native state, I hope you will some day. In the meantime, sit back with a cup of coffee or herbal tea and enjoy your make-believe visit as you read *Virginia Hearts.*

May God bless you and the ones that are near to your heart!

Cordially in Christ,
Tamela

THE ELUSIVE
MR. PERFECT

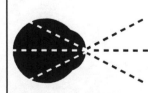

This Large Print Book carries the
Seal of Approval of N.A.V.H.

*To my wonderful family and many friends
in Virginia.
Y'all will always be close to my heart.*

CHAPTER 1

"An exhilarating night with the swinging singles — all six of us." Joelle Jamison's feet, clad in athletic shoes, dragged through the graveled area that served as the church parking lot. The time was 9:30, and the group had already broken up for the night.

Reaching to toss her hair over her shoulder in her favorite expression of disdain, Joelle was reminded she had recently traded her long mane for chin-length locks. Her straight blond hair had been mussed for an uncombed look. Contrary to its freewheeling appearance, though, the style was cemented with hair wax and a coat of ultimate-hold spray. After a week with the new do, she already entertained fantasies of growing it out into a controlled bob.

"Six people isn't so bad. At least we had an even number." Dean grinned, flashing straight, even teeth. Joelle couldn't help remembering four years of braces for him, and two for her. Both could thank Dr. Hart for their brilliant smiles.

Joelle smiled without exposing the orthodontist's handiwork. "Oh, I'm sure you and Zach were happy to be outnumbered by us women."

Dean arched an auburn eyebrow. "Sure gave us an advantage in the sports category of that trivia game."

"As if that were the only advantage," Joelle quipped.

He chuckled as he held open the passenger door of the silver hand-me-down family sedan for Joelle. "The balance at our meeting reminds me of that old Beach Boys song — 'Two Girls for Every Boy.' Sounds ideal to me." He chuckled.

"You had the advantage this week, but we might have more women next week, and you'll be overwhelmed."

"I doubt it," Dean answered. "We're lucky even six people showed up."

"Really? You've got to be kidding!" Joelle wriggled into the blue seat. She felt pampered by Dean's gesture of opening the door, even though she didn't expect him to act the gentleman around her. Joelle had been best friends with Dean Nichols since they shared a bag of chocolate chip cookies the first day of preschool. Instead of acting

10

as though he'd known her all his life, he remained gallant, as though he were still trying to impress her.

"I'm not kidding. There are usually only five of us, and I get the feeling Zach didn't mind you as an addition to our happy little group." With a muscular arm, Dean slammed the door shut. The old hinge objected with a creak. Joelle imagined herself a sardine, shut in a tin can for good . . . only instead of basking in mustard sauce or olive oil, she was enveloped in a musty odor emitted by moisture trapped in the cloth seats, typical of aged cars that had never been garaged.

Joelle waited until he jumped behind the wheel before she responded. "Zach and me? You've got to be kidding." She grimaced. "He's nice, but all he talks is sports. Just not my type. Anyway, didn't you see how Ashlynn was flirting with him?"

"Yeah," he admitted. "She brushed up on football all winter, and now she's trying to learn the ins and outs of baseball. Pun intended." Dean's lips curled into a smile of satisfaction as he pulled out of the lot.

"Oh, you're so brilliant." Joelle's tone indicated she didn't wish to be interpreted literally. "As much fun as I had, even you have to admit the group could use a few more people."

"You didn't really expect fifty singles when our church only has a hundred members, did you? It's not like we live in New York City."

She picked up on his disparaging tone. "You mean Gotham?"

"Some people call it that. And for good reason, I'm sure." Dean let down his window. "I'll take our little community anytime over hordes of people trying to beat each other in the rat race."

Following Dean's lead, Joelle pressed the button to lower her window. The spring day had turned into a cool night. The outdoors smelled of new blossoms and freshly cut grass.

"You won't get that kind of atmosphere in any city."

Joelle inhaled deeply. "True. Living in the mountains does have its merits, even if a large gene pool isn't one of them." She studied his profile, noting his familiar pointed nose. "Don't you get tired of the same people, week after week after week?"

"I never seem to get tired of you."

"But it's different with friends," she protested.

"Is it?" Dean wondered. Joelle was contemplating his point when he continued.

"Who needs a lot of crazy people, when you can only marry one person?"

"One at any given time, anyway." Joelle kept her expression serious, just to see how Dean would react.

"If I didn't know you better . . ." Taking one hand off the wheel for a moment, Dean wagged his index finger at her in mock derision.

She couldn't hold back a rollicking laugh. Joelle could make light of such notions now. Before she responded to Pastor Brown's invitation to accept Jesus Christ as her personal Savior six months ago, she might have been a wee bit serious.

Jokes about Gotham aside, Joelle knew firsthand that one didn't have to live in a big city to find trouble.

"Speaking of crazy people, has that jerk ever stopped calling you?" Dean wanted to know.

"By 'that jerk,' do you mean Dustin?"

"Unless you have more than one jerk in your life."

"Thankfully not." She chuckled. "But I haven't seen Dustin lately."

"Good. You let me know if he bothers you again."

"You're so cute in your knight's shining armor, Sir Dean."

"How true. And don't you forget it."

Dean pulled into Mary's, an eatery the locals had affectionately dubbed "The Greasy Spoon." Mary's provided rickety cane chairs, kitchen noises that could be heard by every customer, and paneled walls covered with watercolor pictures bearing price tags, courtesy of a local artist. Out of habit more than interest, Joelle picked up two free copies of *Today's Southwest Virginian Christian Singles* from a rack at the entrance. Since the dinner rush was past, they quickly found seats. She handed Dean his paper as soon as they ordered a round of banana cream pie and coffee.

Dean glanced at the front-page headline. "Looks like the walk-a-thon was a success."

Joelle nodded. "It says here they raised almost two thousand dollars for the hospice." Her interest satisfied, she flipped through the circular, passing advertisements for religious bookstores and businesses owned and operated by Christians. Announcements of church-sponsored concerts and seminars were plentiful. She pointed to an ad. "Here's a seminar on Managing Finances According to Godly Principles." She looked up at her companion. "Maybe they can tell you how to save for that new car you've been wanting."

"New car? They'd probably tell me to keep old Vicky." Dean contradicted his words by leaning over to take a closer look at the page Joelle held open.

"I don't know. Looks like they have a lot of experts scheduled. May be worthwhile." She glanced into his hazel eyes. "What do you think?"

"I think I'll start practicing godly principles by staying home instead of wasting fuel driving to Raleigh."

"Suit yourself." She shrugged before flipping to the back of the paper. The word *Personals* jumped out at her. "When did they start carrying personal ads?"

Dean took a swig of coffee. "Who knows? I never saw them before. Then again, I wasn't looking." He picked up his copy and located the ads. "Listen to this: 'Wanted, Single Female, for days of hiking in the mountains, walks in the rain, and nights of gourmet meals accompanied by the strains of Mozart and Bach.' "

"What's so bad about that?"

"I'm just wondering who'll be cooking the gourmet meals."

"You've got a point."

Dean scanned the page and teased, "I found the ad you placed, Joelle. 'Beautiful single female with excellent build, variety of hobbies, interested in exploring her walk of faith. Looking for a godly man ready for a true commitment.' "

"Thanks for the compliment, but with such high demands, that ad seems to be courting disappointment." She scanned the page. "This one must be yours: 'Handsome single male with outstanding physique, ready for any challenge. Godly, unafraid of commitment, light on baggage.' "

"You caught me." Picking up a white paper napkin, Dean waved it in surrender.

Joelle chuckled.

Dean balled up his napkin and tossed it on his dessert plate. "Just for the sake of argument, let's say that was my ad. Question is, if I'm so wonderful, then why do I need to advertise?"

"Because you only see five other unmarried people every week, and one of them is a guy? Like, duh!" She rolled her eyes. "Seriously, some of these singles don't seem so pitiful. A few might even be fun. Maybe answering one or two of these ads wouldn't be such a bad idea."

Dean placed his coffee cup on the table with a firm motion and leaned toward her. "Please say you're joking. You've got to know these people are losers. They're making up half of what they say, and the other half isn't true. It's a dangerous world out there."

"I know. But everyone in here is a Christian, right?"

"Or so they say," he answered.

"They're screened, right?"

Returning his attention to the paper, Dean studied the headings. "I don't see anything about that. All I see is a disclaimer saying the paper takes no responsibility for any contacts made."

"They've got to say that to keep out of court. There's always somebody ready to file a lawsuit in hopes of making a fast buck."

"Then don't take a chance by responding to these ads. Take my word for it, Joelle. You'll regret it."

Unwilling to argue further, Joelle shrugged. Dean might be her best friend, but he wasn't going to tell her what to do. Rolling up the paper, she slipped it into her denim shoulder bag. As soon as she got home, Joelle planned to comb the entries and select her next date.

CHAPTER 2

Two Saturdays later, Joelle waited for Prince Charming to arrive.

"What time is Lloyd supposed to get here?" her mother asked.

"Seven."

Eleanor Jamison looked toward the surrealistic clock on the kitchen wall. The words "Does It Matter?" and scrambled numbers decorated its face. "It's only six-thirty and you're set to go already? This guy must be something special. Is he from your singles' group at church?"

Joelle shook her head. "He lives two counties away."

"Oh." Eleanor's voice rose with inflection, but she continued wiping the breakfast nook table clean.

Joelle was relieved her mother's curiosity was satisfied. Since her job as a doctor's bookkeeper and billing clerk allowed Joelle to meet people from around the region, the explanation seemed logical. Joelle knew if a relationship developed, she could always give her mother more details about how she and Lloyd Newby really met. Later. Much later.

Joelle rose from the couch. "Can I help you with anything?"

Eleanor's gaze swept over her daughter. "I wouldn't think of asking you to do housework when you've got on such a nice outfit. Besides, I'm caught up. All I need to do is study."

Eleanor's schoolwork had been woven into the Jamisons' family life for the past couple of months. Joelle was proud that her mother was being tutored for her GED test. "Do you need me to call out questions or anything while I wait?"

"Nope. It's math. I'm just going to review some problems to make sure I understand them."

"I don't see how you do it, Mom. Working full time, then studying for your GED."

"It's not easy, but it's something I have to do. Just for myself. Besides, I'll earn my diploma soon enough." She let out a sigh. "I had no business dropping out of school to marry your father. Your grandparents tried to talk us out of it, but we were too much in love. Besides, I hated school and wanted to work."

"And then Benjamin came along and ruined your career." Joelle chuckled as she thought about her boisterous brother.

"Believe me, I was glad to exchange assembly line work for mounds of diapers. I was too naïve to realize how easy school was in comparison to working every day of the week. Two years of sorting buttons at the factory was about all I could take."

"Harder than sorting out all the fights among the five of us, huh?"

Smiling, Eleanor shook her head. "I won't go that far, but I'm just glad none of you kids followed my poor example, at least as far as your education goes. You were smart to graduate from high school, and now you're smart to wait for marriage, Joelle." Eleanor took a seat at the table and flipped open her book. "Although, since you've seen your twenty-ninth birthday, I just hope you're not being too smart for your own good."

"I doubt I'll ever be that smart." Joelle tried not to flinch. Her mother's words hit too close to home.

Eleanor didn't seem to notice Joelle's discomfort. "Not that anything in life is easy, mind you. Back then, if not for the Lord's mercy, I wouldn't have made it. He sure must have been looking after me."

"I think He was. And He still is."

Joelle picked up the day's newspaper. Her eyes refused to focus on the print. Instead, she imagined what Lloyd Newby must be like in person. He had seemed nice enough on the telephone when he called to set up the date. He said he attended church almost every Sunday and was a Christian. Even so, if a relationship developed, she dreaded the day she'd have to admit she met Lloyd through a personal ad. The fact it appeared in a Christian paper would have comforted her parents about as much as it had Dean — which wasn't much at all.

Joelle's thoughts wandered to her best friend. When she had turned down his invitation to tonight's singles' meeting at church, Dean guessed the reason. Though he didn't express outright opposition, the crestfallen expression on his face revealed his disappointment so much, she almost relented. But she didn't. And now she fought pangs of guilt.

Dean knows I can see him anytime. He should understand.

Confident in that knowledge, Joelle put Dean out of her mind. Stealing a glance at her mother, Joelle could see the older woman was absorbed in her work. She sneaked the clipped ad out of her purse and studied it:

A rare combination in one package: charming, cosmopolitan, and Christian! Open-minded, handsome bachelor, 25, seeks fun-loving Christian bachelorette, 22–32. My favorite things are candlelight dinners, moonlit walks, and travel to exotic locales. Want to see London? Rome? Paris? Then I'm the man for you. Ooo — la la!

He's perfect! Joelle felt a triumphant smile touch her lips. *Handsome, Christian, and with promises of travel, he must be rich, too. How could Dean possibly object? If anything, he should be happy for me.*

As if on cue, the unobjectionable Lloyd Newby rang the bell. Joelle heard her father's voice. He must have just returned from feeding the small herd of beef cattle that supplemented his income as a teacher. Joseph Jamison was speaking to Lloyd in a kind yet no-nonsense manner. Taking the opportunity to rush to the bathroom, Joelle indulged in one last check of her appearance.

Joelle always chose to avoid cosmetics. Her clear complexion and blushing pink lips required no enhancement. The only vanity she allowed herself was a pair of aqua-colored contact lenses to conceal light brown eyes she judged to be blah. Once the contacts were in place, the bolt of blue-green on her irises was so astounding that the artifice was evident even to the casual observer. Nevertheless, the lenses made Joelle feel beautiful enough to conquer any situation.

Lloyd hadn't told Joelle about his plans for the evening but to trust him that she would enjoy herself. Joelle knew her crisp white blouse, shaped by princess seams, and a slim pair of black pants with matching flats would take her in style to the restaurant and to most other places he might suggest. Classic pearl stud earrings and one strand of small pearls hanging an inch below the hollow of her throat added warm luster.

When she was convinced her father had had enough time to visit with Lloyd, Joelle set her shoulders back and strode into the living room for her entrance.

"Joelle?" A look of relief crossed Lloyd's face.

A quick glance at her father's furrowed brow revealed he wondered why Lloyd didn't recognize her. Joelle made a point of focusing on her date. She flashed him a smile. "That's me." Lloyd looked much as he promised during their one brief phone conversation — a tall blond his friends described as good-looking. "Dad and you are getting acquainted, I see."

"Sure are," Joseph chuckled, extending his hand to his daughter's date. "It was nice to meet you, Lloyd."

"You too, sir."

Cutting her glance to the den's entrance, Joelle noticed her mother peering into the room. Eleanor's reassuring smile comforted Joelle.

The door had barely shut behind the couple when Lloyd inquired, "Does your father interrogate everyone who comes to see you, or does he have something against me because of the way we met?"

Joelle felt her heart leap in fear. "You didn't tell him about that, did you?"

"About my ad? Of course not." His eyebrows shot up. "You mean to say, he doesn't already know?"

She shook her head with force, though not enough to disturb her waxed curls.

"In that case, I feel sorry for every guy that crosses your threshold." His lips twisted. "I wasn't expecting to meet parents. Aren't you a little old to still be living at home?"

24

She bristled. "I don't think so." Already on the defensive, she wasn't about to share her life story with Lloyd. Joelle made no further comment as she watched Lloyd stride to his side of his new car, a model she didn't recognize, without opening the door for her.

Dean would have opened the door for me.

Forcing the unwelcome thought from her mind, Joelle slid into the passenger seat, wondering what to say next. She needn't have worried.

"I must say, you look quite lovely. Even better than you described yourself."

His compliment caused Joelle to soften her stance. "I'm glad I didn't disappoint."

"You didn't. Trust me on that. But I had hoped you would appear in something a little more dressy, a little more upscale."

"Oh?" Joelle noticed he was wearing a black turtleneck under a blazer even though the warm spring weather hardly required a coat. A twinge of embarrassment turned to irritation, though she tried to keep her voice sweet. "Why didn't you say something? I would have changed."

He shrugged. "Never mind. I'm sure they'll let us in."

Before she could retort, he began chattering away about travel. Through a series of monologues, Lloyd relived every vacation he'd ever taken, down to the last detail. He expressed his sense of adventure in his plans to travel to Fiji, Australia, and Borneo. His enthusiasm lasted through the fifty-mile drive to Roanoke. Though she was used to more give-and-take in conversation, Joelle had to admit that hearing him talk about places she'd never been was riveting.

As Lloyd handed his car keys to the valet, he told her he had ordered Chateaubriand when he made the reservations. He explained, "The dish, filet mignon beef with béarnaise sauce, is usually shared by two people. Since the filet is large, the restaurant requires patrons to order Chateaubriand ahead to allow extra preparation time."

Joelle couldn't help but be impressed. Obviously, Lloyd was accustomed to eating well.

They were seated at an intimate table set with a linen tablecloth, gold-trimmed china, fine silverware, and several etched glasses. Large chandeliers hung from the ceiling. Each light bulb was covered by a small lampshade. Joelle had forgotten the month of May was prom season. High school students, dressed in colorful gowns and tuxedos, occupied several tables. Joelle wished she hadn't chosen to wear her black pants, dressy though they were.

Lloyd no longer seemed to mind how she was dressed. He relished taking charge, even placing her order along with his, from the first course to the last. Joelle thought perhaps she should object to Lloyd's presumptuousness. She was debating whether or not to speak up when she realized his willingness to tend to such details left her feeling relaxed.

Until the first course.

Six tiny phyllo dough pastries were placed before her. She guessed the filling inside wasn't chocolate.

Lloyd placed his napkin in his lap. "The escargot is especially good here."

"Escargot?" Joelle tried to remember the meaning of the French word. "You mean, snails?"

"Of course. The chef makes his own phyllo dough." He lifted his fork and used it to point to the pastries. "And see how moist it looks? That's butter. And, of course, it's seasoned with garlic."

Joelle tried not to grimace.

"What's the matter? You don't like escargot?" Furrowed brows signaled his disappointment.

"'To tell you the truth, I've never tried it before."

"If you want to travel around the world, you'd better get used to sampling foods you don't normally eat."

"I suppose you have a point." With her fork, she prodded through several layers of thin pastry that reminded her of onionskin paper. Though the dough proved scrumptious, Joelle wasn't as pleased with the warm, chewy morsel inside.

"What do you think?"

She swallowed. "Not much taste. It's the same consistency as fried clams, only a little less rubbery."

"Fried clams? I'd expect to find that on a diner menu." He cringed as though she had confessed a penchant for feasting on dodo bird feathers while sitting in a pigsty. He pointed the tines of his fork at his plate. Placed decoratively upon it were thin slices of smoked salmon, trout, and pieces of pheasant on a few leaves of lettuce, sprinkled with capers and a dash of caviar. "Would you like to trade with me?"

Regarding her snails once more, Joelle knew she'd have trouble indulging in even a second pastry. She studied his plate of untouched food. "I'm not too sure about the pheasant." The bird looked like tuna showered with small peas.

He flashed an amused smile. "I'll take

that, and you can have the fish."

"Sounds like a good deal. As long as you don't mind."

"Of course not. Escargot should be eaten by one who appreciates it."

Joelle was thankful the rest of the meal wasn't so daring. A house salad was followed by carrot soup seasoned with ginger, then the Chateaubriand. A smooth chocolate soufflé topped off the meal. Afterward, Joelle felt as though she had just dined at the table of King Louis XIV.

"I've never eaten so much yet not felt stuffed," Joelle observed as she placed her napkin beside her dessert plate. "The meal was excellent, Lloyd."

"Good." A self-satisfied smile flashed over his face as he handed his credit card to the waiter. "There will be more of the same with me, *mon cherie*."

Wanting the experience to last a few moments longer, Joelle savored each drop of rich coffee left in her cup. She had just finished the last sumptuous sip when the waiter returned to the table and mumbled something to Lloyd as he returned the card.

Lloyd crooked one eyebrow. "I can't believe it." As the waiter watched, Lloyd withdrew his wallet and fumbled through several credit cards before handing him a platinum-colored plate. "I'm so sorry. Try this one."

Joelle was grateful another waiter offered her more coffee, giving her a reason simply to nod rather than to speak.

"I do apologize to you, Joelle. How embarrassing."

"Oh, banks make mistakes all the time." Joelle hoped her assurances were more convincing to her date than they were to herself.

She had almost finished her second cup of coffee when the waiter returned, his lips tightened into a severe line. Joelle knew he would tell Lloyd the second card had failed to clear. She caught the words "credit limit exceeded" from their whispered discussion.

"I assure you, I am shocked and appalled." Lloyd's slack-jawed expression and shrill tone of voice matched his professed indignation. "We shall settle this. If you will give us a few moments, please."

Sending them a curt nod, the waiter left his side. Joelle noticed he kept a close watch on their table as he went about his other duties.

"Joelle, again, I apologize. I have no idea why both of my platinum cards were rejected."

She recalled a similar incident with her

own cards, so Joelle wasn't about to judge Lloyd. "It can happen to the best of us."

A half-grin crossed his face. "Thank you for being so understanding. Let me assure you, those banks will be hearing from me first thing Monday morning." Folding his arms across his expanded chest, Lloyd nodded once for emphasis.

"So what do we do now?"

Releasing his arms, Lloyd clenched his teeth and raised his eyebrows. "You wouldn't happen to have any cash on you, would you?"

Joelle remembered she had tucked an extra twenty-dollar bill in her purse in case of an emergency. "Like, how much?"

He reviewed the bill. "It's one hundred, fifty-eight dollars and eighty cents."

She felt her jaw drop open in shock. "Come again?"

"I said, one hundred, fifty-eight dollars and eighty cents." His eyes met hers. "And, of course, a 20 percent tip is expected at a place like this. Always."

She wasn't able to contain her shock, though she was careful to keep her voice barely above a whisper. "How could two people have possibly racked up such a bill?"

Lloyd laid the receipt on the center of the table so she could see for herself:

1 Escargot	$ 9.95
1 Smoked Fish	$10.95
2 Soup	$13.90
2 Salad	$13.90
1 Chateaubriand	$90.00
1 Chocolate Soufflé	$10.95
1 Raspberry Soufflé	$10.95
2 Coffee	$ 5.90
Total	$166.50

Joelle swallowed. "And that doesn't even include tax."

"Thirty-five dollars should be a sufficient tip," he suggested. "Why don't we make it two hundred and ten dollars?"

"Why not make it two hundred and twenty-five dollars?" Joelle couldn't keep the sarcasm out of her tone.

"Look, I said I'm sorry. It's not like I forced you to eat here, you know —"

"Oh, yeah?"

Lloyd leaned closer. "Are you saying you didn't enjoy your meal?"

"No, but —"

"Besides, I'll pay you back. I promise." Lloyd let his spine touch his chair and folded his arms across his chest.

Reaching into her black satin purse, Joelle was thankful she was conservative enough that her own card wasn't maxed out. "I guess I have no other choice, unless I want to wash dishes."

"I said I'd pay you back." Lloyd didn't bother to hide his irritation. He extracted a black leather billfold from his pocket and handed her a twenty-dollar bill. "See? We haven't even left the restaurant yet, and I'm already paying the first installment."

His willingness to pay even that much made Joelle wish to give him the benefit of the doubt. "All right. Thanks."

The ride home was hardly as chatty as the trip to the restaurant had been. Joelle tried to keep the atmosphere pleasant. She forced herself to concentrate on Matthew 5:42: *"Give to him that asketh thee, and from him that would borrow of thee turn not thou away."*

The verse was still rolling in her brain when the car coasted to a stop. Reacting quickly, Lloyd managed to steer it onto the side of the road.

"What happened?"

"I'm not sure." He turned the ignition, but the engine didn't even turn over. Lloyd stared at the gauges. "Uh-oh. I must have run out of gas."

"Run out of gas?" Joelle felt a mixture of irritation and fear.

"I guess I wasn't paying attention. Sorry,"

he answered as though he really didn't mean the apology. "Do you know how far the next gas station is?"

"It should be a mile or two from here."

"Hope you enjoy walking." Lloyd pulled the door lever to let himself out.

"Do I have a choice?"

"Sure. You can stay here by yourself."

"No, thanks." Joelle looked down at her flat shoes and couldn't resist a dig. "Looks like I was right to dress casually after all."

As they walked in silence, Joelle thought about how the spring night, lit by a full moon, would have been enjoyed much more had she been with the right person . . . whomever that was.

Mr. Wrong broke the silence. "Um, I hate to impose on you further, but — well, would you mind all that much if I asked you for my twenty dollars back?"

"You've got to be kidding." Joelle hadn't meant to be uncharitable, but at the moment, her shock was greater than her tact. "Look, I'm sorry. Of course you can have the money."

He jerked the bill from her grasp. "Thanks."

More of Jesus' words struck her mind. *"And if any man will sue thee at the law, and take away thy coat, let him have thy cloak*

34

also. And whosoever shall compel thee to go a mile, go with him twain."

"You're welcome," Joelle managed as the glare of headlamps lit their backs. Turning, she recognized Dean's car.

Oh, no! I can't let Dean see me like this! Bowing her head, Joelle stared at the ground just ahead of her feet. Maybe Dean wouldn't recognize her and would drive past.

Instead, the car slowed down and pulled over just ahead of them.

Lloyd halted in his tracks and grabbed Joelle's elbow, clutching it in a viselike grip. "I don't like this. Whoever's in that car could be some maniac, and we're easy prey."

"That's no maniac. That's my best friend."

CHAPTER 3

Dean squinted as his car approached a couple walking along the edge of the mountain road. He'd spotted an automobile abandoned about a half-mile back and wondered about its owners. They had to be strangers. Nobody he knew possessed such an exotic import. Dean figured the couple and the car belonged together.

Stopping for strangers on the roadside wasn't his habit, but the night sky threatened rain, and there was little chance they'd be able to walk to the next gas station before getting drenched. Dean knew he'd want someone to do him a similar kindness should he ever become stranded.

Slowing to a stop, Dean recognized the woman's lithe figure. His heart did a funny flip-flop. "Is that you, Joelle?"

The sweet voice he could have distinguished from thousands of others answered. "It's me." Joelle bowed her head and stared at the ground.

Her companion wasn't so shy, boring a hole into Dean with his eyes. Dean's lips tightened when he realized the tall, blond man was Joelle's reason for cutting out of Singles' Night. Meeting the stare of his competition, Dean didn't note anything special. Since his fancy car broke down, maybe Joelle wouldn't, either. He forced himself to smile as he exited his car.

After making introductions, Joelle took her place beside Dean. Lloyd, lips curled downward in a pout, plopped himself in the backseat.

"Did your car break down?" Dean asked.

"Of course not," Lloyd snapped. "It's just out of gas."

The solution was obvious to Dean. Ever since his fuel gauge became stuck on the halfway mark a couple of years ago, he had made a habit of keeping a can of gas in his trunk. "Not a problem. I've got a gallon —" He interrupted himself when he saw Joelle shaking her head in short, quick motions.

Lloyd's face brightened. "You've got some here in the car? Great!"

"That's okay, Dean," Joelle said. "Lloyd can pay for his own gas."

"I don't mind."

"He said he doesn't mind," Lloyd agreed.

Dean wondered why Joelle didn't want him to help her date out of the bind. Whatever her reasons, her protests were too late. Dean had made the offer, and he wasn't about to back down. After depositing the fuel into Lloyd's car, Dean made sure the car started before bidding them both good-bye. Lloyd didn't offer to pay, and Dean didn't ask. He didn't mind. It was the least he could do for Joelle.

As Dean pulled away, Joelle waved. To his satisfaction, she looked miserable.

The following Monday, Dean was on his way home when his cell phone rang. He let out a sigh. *What else can go wrong today?*

He had already repaired two washing machines in one of the three Laundromats he owned. Counting today, that would make three repairs in the past month. He'd have to replace at least one machine soon, and two dryers were threatening to expire.

Despite the hassles, Dean was proud of the business he called his own. He had sunk every cent into buying the Laundromats when Mr. Chaney retired. Even then, the older man had given him a price break because he knew Dean well.

Dean had prayed about the purchase. He knew being an entrepreneur offered independence but carried a stiff price in responsibility. When Dean felt the Lord's leading to go forward with the purchase, he vowed to honor Him by being a good steward. One way was to offer his customers dependable machines. That meant not keeping those that were sputtering to a slow, lingering death, no matter how tempting the urge — or the need — to save money might be.

Dean made sure his facilities were clean. He was thankful his sister, Mandy, didn't mind the job. The small salary from Dean gave her a sense of freedom and his brother-in-law a couple of evenings a week to spend time with their two boys.

As he answered the phone, Dean expected to hear Mandy's voice, telling him about something gone awry at the site she was cleaning. If disaster was in the making, that would mean a round trip of eighty miles added to the end of an exhausting day. "Wash 'n Wear," he murmured, trying not to sound too depressed.

"Hi, Dean."

"Joelle!" His sigh of relief was audible. "Am I glad it's you."

She giggled. "You were expecting Mandy."

"How well you know." Dean remembered he was supposed to be mad at Joelle for dumping him on Singles' Night to go off with that snob she met through the personals, of all places. "I saw yesterday in church you got home all right from your date."

"I want to talk to you about that." Joelle's voice was a combination of mockery and teasing. "I tried to catch up with you after Sunday school, but you were off faster than I could shake a stick."

"An emergency at one of the stores. Water gushing all over the place." Dean cringed at the memory.

"Sorry. Well, at least it's fixed now." She paused a moment. "I want to thank you properly for stopping for Lloyd and me. How about dinner at Mary's tonight? My treat. Have you got time?"

Of course I have time for you, he wanted to say. Instead, he answered, "I think so."

"Good. Besides, isn't getting together what friends do?"

Friends. He had grown to hate that word. Sometimes Dean wondered if Joelle's lack of romantic feelings toward him was his own fault. After all, he hadn't said anything to lead Joelle to believe he loved her as more than a friend. He wanted to. Badly. But he couldn't. She was so vulnerable right now.

Dean had been at church with Joelle six months ago when she responded to the call to accept Christ as her personal Savior.

Otherwise, he might not have believed it. Joelle had seemed perfectly content with her life. The youngest of five, she lived comfortably with her parents and never mentioned any desire to leave — except for once, a few years ago. After only a few months on her own, she returned, older and wiser.

And certainly now she was richer. He remembered the day Joelle pulled into his driveway in her new sports car. He'd been astounded that she had paid cash for it. As a child, Joelle had enjoyed few luxuries. When she became a young adult, Joelle developed a habit of splurging whenever she had money, and sometimes when she didn't. Pride in material possessions kept her on top of the world for awhile. But as debts piled high and her new possessions aged, Dean could see Joelle develop a longing for something deeper. She'd gone to school and grown responsible. She'd even told him about her yearning to meet a man she could settle down with, someone who wasn't afraid to commit.

Under other circumstances, Dean would have made it clear she'd already met that man. Only at that point, Joelle hadn't made the decision to accept the Lord. She was comfortable keeping Christ in the background, a benign figure who loved her and who would always be there.

Jesus was much more to Dean. He never made an important decision without consulting the Lord. That kind of prayer life wasn't something Joelle practiced. Even now, she would need time to develop a full relationship with the Savior. Dean didn't want to interfere with that.

He remembered 2 Corinthians 6:14: *"Be ye not unequally yoked together with unbelievers: for what fellowship hath righteousness with unrighteousness? and what communion hath light with darkness?"*

No way would he spend his life unequally yoked. Not even for Joelle.

But then she made the decision.

Joelle's voice brought him back to the present. "How about tonight?"

"Tonight?"

She must have noticed he seemed distracted. "If that's not good —"

"No, that's fine." He glanced at the clock on the dashboard. "I can be at your house at seven."

After they hung up, Dean found himself whistling a tuneless melody. The reason Joelle wanted to see him didn't matter. What mattered was, she wanted to be with him.

■ ■ ■ ■

"So what I want you to do, Dean, is help me find someone else."

Dean nearly dropped his cup of coffee. "Say what?"

"You heard me. I want you to help me find someone else."

He looked straight into her eyes. The teal contact lenses were a perfect match for the soft turquoise sweater she wore. After experimenting with hair flipped upward, on this day Joelle had styled her golden locks in a sleek fashion. He liked the effect. In fact, Dean was sure he was the only man who could appreciate Joelle. Why would she waste her time with anyone else? He didn't bother to hide his irritation. "After what you told me about that lousy date? Surely you can't mean you want to try again, Joelle."

"So?" She shrugged.

Dean snapped his fingers in front of her nose. "Joelle, time to wake up."

She laughed. "I'm perfectly awake, thank you."

"In that case, what planet are you from, and what did you do with Joelle?"

A chuckle was her only answer.

Dean shook his head. "Joelle, I know how much you value your money. It's not like you to throw away hundreds of dollars with such a cavalier attitude."

"But I've accepted Christ now. Like you always tell me, all earthly things belong to Him. Anyway, in the scheme of things, it was probably a good investment," she said. "I learned more about myself and what's really important."

"True," he admitted.

"Besides, Lloyd said he'd pay me back."

"Sort of like he paid you that first twenty dollars, huh?"

Joelle flinched. "Maybe he was just having a bad night. We'll see."

"Yes, we will. I'll tell you one thing. If I were a betting man, I'd gamble he won't pay you back. You'll never see him again." Dean took a sip of coffee. "Wonder how many other women he's taken advantage of like that?"

"Who knows? All I know is, I learned my lesson. I guess I was trying to be too greedy. Would you believe that verse we talked about in class a couple of Sundays ago kept popping into my head?"

" 'Give to him that asketh thee, and from him that would borrow of thee turn not thou away.' That one?"

She nodded.

"You wouldn't have been so nonchalant about this a year ago." He felt his eyes grow misty. "I can see the Lord really is starting to work in your life."

"He must have been there all along, to send me a friend like you."

Friend. There's that word again. Dean gazed into the face he loved, the one sending an angelic smile in his direction. He wished he were a painter so he could capture the rose flush of her cheeks, her lips the color of a strawberry milk shake, her lustrous golden hair. No photograph could portray such glory with any accuracy.

"What are you thinking?" she asked.

"You don't want to know."

She opened her mouth as if in protest, but something stopped her. Instead, she reached for the latest issue of *Today's Southwest Virginian Christian Singles.* He narrowed his eyes. He wished Joelle had never seen that paper. If only she had given him time . . . time to let her get used to the real presence of the Lord in her life.

Dean hadn't wanted to pursue Joelle when she was so vulnerable, at the point when she had approached the fork in the road and had chosen the right path. The narrow path. He had visualized himself helping her along the way, guiding her at times, walking beside her at other times, perhaps her even leading him on still other occasions. Now, because he had waited for her instead of pouncing, he was being asked to help her find someone else.

"No!" he blurted. His outburst was strong enough to elicit stares from the women at the adjacent table. Dean recognized one of them as a member of his mom's garden club. From the corner of his eye, he noticed they suddenly huddled together and whispered. He didn't even care.

A stricken expression flashed into Joelle's eyes. "No, what?"

He lowered his voice. "No, I'm not going to help you ruin your life. Wasn't one bad date enough?"

"Enough with him, yes, but I won't pick someone like that this time."

Seeing there was no use in trying to talk sense into Joelle, Dean extracted a twenty-dollar bill from his wallet and threw it on the table.

"Wait! I said it was my treat."

He was in no mood to take any gift from Joelle. "You can pay me back some other time." Slipping out of the booth, he headed for the exit without saying another word.

As he made his way to the car, he heard

Joelle's footfalls crunching on the gravel behind him. Dean almost wished he could leave her standing there, but he opened the door on her side, catching a whiff of her floral perfume that saturated the inside of the car.

Dean sighed. It would be a long ride home.

Joelle allowed silence to permeate the car. From time to time, she would steal a furtive look at Dean's profile, the straight nose, strong chin, and full lips she knew so well. He kept his eyes focused straight ahead. The road curved around in several hairpin turns, challenging even the best driver. Dean had navigated it so many times over his life, Joelle knew he hardly needed to concentrate. His anger filled the space between them. If she could draw a caricature of Dean at that moment, she would include a thundercloud over his head.

Just before they reached her driveway, Joelle knew she would have to be the one to break the oppressive stillness. "What's the matter with you, Dean? Don't you want me to be happy?"

"Of course I want you to be happy." His gruff tone would have put off a lesser friend.

"You don't seem like it."

"Things aren't always as they seem."

"What's that supposed to mean?"

He pulled the car up to the flagstone walk leading to her front door. "It means I won't go through that paper and pick your next date."

"All right. You don't have to." She stepped out of the car. "I can fend for myself."

He leaned toward her, his auburn hair catching the light from the porch. "Can you? Remember that the next time you're stranded."

Despite the edge in his voice, Joelle stood in place, waiting for him to kill the engine and walk her to the door, as was his custom. Instead, Dean drove off, leaving behind a cloud of red dust as he sped over the dirt road.

Her gray mutt ran up, leapt, and placed her front paws on the side of Joelle's leg, barking happily. Without taking her gaze from the departing car, Joelle gave Raindrop a pat on the head. "What could possibly be the matter with him?"

CHAPTER 4

NO FRILLS, JUST SIMPLE PLEA-
SURES. Devout Sunday school teacher,
35, seeks Christian woman, 25–35, who
enjoys quiet evenings at home reading
fine books and listening to classical music.
If you're cerebral and quality time with an
equally cerebral, attractive man sounds
good to you, I'm the one you've been
seeking!

Scanning her latest copy of *Today's Southwest Virginian Christian Singles,* Joelle
stopped at the ad. As she munched on a
tuna salad sandwich, strawberry yogurt, and
soda, she read in relative privacy behind the
closed door of her office. Even better, her
next date would likely be at work. She could
quickly leave a message on his answering
machine and get back to sending out the
month's bills.

She read the ad one last time as she picked

up the phone to dial the number listed. A Sunday school teacher! Even if the ad hadn't included the word "devout," the fact that this man was willing to teach a class every Sunday was good enough for her. Not even Dean could argue against a Sunday school teacher. Surely this new man was an unimpeachable Christian.

Joelle thought about the other specifications. Maybe "cerebral" wasn't the first adjective to describe her, but Joelle thought her grades in school had been good enough. Maybe classical music wasn't her first choice, but she could usually sit still through at least a couple of the unbearably lengthy compositions before turning the station to something more contemporary. Surely she wouldn't disappoint this brainiac. And surely he would prove a far cry from the world-class sponger she had chosen for her last date. Shuddering at the thought, Joelle had no time to dwell on her past failure before someone answered the ringing phone. "Hello?"

Joelle was taken aback by the fact that the voice belonged to a female, but she rebounded before her surprise became evident. "Is this the number where I might reach Dexter Smythe?"

"Who wants to know?" The voice sounded

edgy, suspicious.

I hope this isn't his roommate!

Joelle's heart beat with anxiety. "Um, I'm calling in reference to the ad."

"Oh! The ad! The one in the Christian singles' magazine?" The voice sounded relieved, then became perky.

"Yes."

"Well, why didn't you say so?" She could hear the woman's smile.

"Um, I did —"

"You know, that ad hasn't gotten the number of responses I had hoped. I think that's because it takes a very special woman in this day and age to shun the glitz and glamour the world has to offer in exchange for an honest, down-to-earth boy like my son, Dexter."

Well, that explained why Joelle was talking to a female. She breathed a sigh of relief before uttering, "Thank you, ma'am."

"My Dexter is a good catch. He knows his way around computers, and everyone knows they're the wave of the future."

Joelle considered computers to be the wave of the present, but she refrained from making the observation.

"So many women are so pushy today. All they seem to want is a man who'll make plenty of money so they can laze about all

51

day and have their nails done." She paused. "You do your own manicures, don't you?"

"Yes, ma'am." Joelle glanced at her unpolished nails that she had trimmed to an attractive length and buffed to a sheen.

"How charming that you keep calling me 'ma'am.' I can tell you were brought up right. But there's no need to 'ma'am' me. Just call me Bertha. And you are . . . ?"

"Joelle."

"Noelle? So you were born at Christmas?"

"No, ma'am. I mean, Bertha. It's Joelle with a J."

"Ah. That is a very unusual name, although it is quite lovely. I take it your father's name is Joe and he really wanted a boy?" Bertha managed to conjecture without sounding offensive.

"No, I have four older brothers. My name is a combination of my parents' names, Joseph and Eleanor." Having spilled so much information so quickly, Joelle realized she had let Bertha lure her into becoming much too chatty.

"Oh. How interesting. So your mom has five children, huh? It's so lovely to learn you come from a family that values tradition and old-fashioned ways. The world moves much too rapidly these days," Bertha opined. "So, Joelle, do you have a last name?"

Despite Bertha's obviously sincere attempts to be pleasant, Joelle was becoming annoyed. Calling a man she'd never met was difficult enough without having to undergo an inquisition from his mother. Nevertheless, she concentrated on making sure her voice revealed no negative feelings. "Jamison. Joelle Jamison."

"How darling! Does anyone call you J. J.?"

"Not as of yet." Joelle drew a breath. "I don't mean to be abrupt, but I really must keep this call short. I'm on my lunch break, and I need to get back to my work in a couple of minutes. If you want to know the truth, I figured an answering machine would take the call so I could just leave my name and number. Since I managed to contact a human" — she giggled in hopes her amusement would be contagious — "I may as well speak to Dexter."

"I'd be glad for you to speak to him, except Dexter's not in."

"Perhaps I could leave my number —"

"That won't be necessary. I know exactly what Dexter would say if he were here," Bertha assured. "He has tickets to Concert under the Stars at the community college. It's on Friday night. The symphony will be playing selections from Mozart and Debussy. You know their works quite well, yes?"

53

"Well enough, I'm sure."

"Good. And don't worry about dinner. Dexter can bring a picnic basket."

"Sounds like fun," Joelle had to admit.

"Oh, it will be!"

After firming up the details and giving directions to her house, Joelle asked, "Why don't I leave my number, just in case Dexter would like to talk to me before we meet?"

"You're welcome to leave your number, but I can tell just from your voice and how polite you are that Dexter will be as crazy about you as I already am."

Friday night, Joelle's hands shook as she popped in her contact lenses as she readied herself for the date. She'd been the victim of friends' matchmaking efforts before, but never had she flown this blind. What had made her agree to go to a concert with a man she hadn't met, or even spoken to?

I wish I could talk to Dean before taking such a plunge. But why? All he'd do is say "I told you so" and add that I should cancel. He might even give me a lecture on going out with strangers, not to mention another reminder that I never should have tried to find someone in a personals ad — even if the magazine is published by and for Christians.

She sighed. Dean hadn't called all week,

and she hadn't been able to manufacture a convincing excuse to phone him. She knew he wasn't pleased that she was trying the ads again, but she never dreamed he wouldn't even speak to her in the interim. For the hundredth time, she wished she could hear his voice . . . even if it was lecturing.

Joelle deliberately focused on the upcoming evening. She glanced at the daisy-shaped clock in her room, a relic from her teen years. Dexter was due in ten minutes. She wondered if he'd be on time. Maybe he'd be inconsiderate, showing up late and making them miss the first part of the concert. She shook her head at the reflection in the dresser mirror. Classical music fan. Cerebral. Sounded like someone who'd have his watch set with precision so he could be exactly on time.

Coaxing hair that hadn't quite reached her shoulders into a manageable bob, Joelle mused that Dexter was lucky her parents were at an annual awards banquet for her mom's work. That meant he wouldn't be subjected to Dad's standard pre-date interview. Not that Dexter didn't deserve it after the examination Bertha had conducted with her. Sighing as she remembered the grilling, Joelle slipped into a pair of denim sandals.

They matched the indigo-washed jeans she wore, which in turn picked up the deep blue roses embroidered on a recent acquisition, a coral short-sleeved summer sweater. Going for cashmere had been a splurge, but the cloud-soft knit was so luxurious, she felt as though any evening would be a success when she was wearing such a garment. Remembering Bertha's comment about manicures, Joelle gave her nails one last swipe with the buffer before her date rang the bell.

"Here goes!" she said to no one in particular. After hurrying through the den and living room, she opened the heavy oak door.

Dexter's ad had promised someone attractive, but the description barely fit the man of slight build who was standing on the front porch. As if to compensate for a receding hairline, he had grown the hair on the back of his head almost to his shoulders. A full beard that hid most of his face looked as though it hadn't been subjected to a pair of scissors in a few months. She felt a sudden urge to braid it but held her face in rigid composure, lest she wrinkle her nose in distaste. Her gaze swept to a nondescript shirt and khaki pants before returning to his face and noting stylish, wire-rimmed eyeglasses. Joelle suspected their removal would not improve his appearance.

Well, he did say he's cerebral, and I remember reading somewhere that geniuses rarely care about their looks. Besides, if I learned nothing else from my date with Lloyd, it's that appearances aren't everything.

"You must be Joelle."

"Good guess." She grinned, but he didn't return her expression.

"Let's go."

Joelle expected Dexter to give her at least a cursory glance and perhaps compliment her appearance. Instead, the command was barely out of his mouth before he turned and led her to a dependable-looking blue car with four doors, its engine still running. She was puzzled by his nonchalance but excused it as shyness. Bertha had mentioned Dexter's love of computers. Perhaps he dealt with machines so much, he had trouble communicating well with people. Besides, there would be time to get to know each other over the course of the evening.

Dexter didn't bother to open the car door for her but hurried to his side and slid behind the wheel.

Is Dean the last man on Earth who still opens car doors for women? Shaking her head, Joelle willed thoughts of Dean out of her mind. This was no time to be thinking

57

of anyone else. She had placed the call to Dexter's house. She owed him a fair chance.

Her thoughts were interrupted by a female voice from the backseat. "Hello, Joelle!"

Joelle's head snapped in the direction of Bertha's now-familiar voice.

Bertha looked nothing as Joelle had imagined. Based on their earlier telephone conversation, she had visualized Bertha in a no-nonsense business suit, probably black or navy blue. Joelle's Bertha wore precision-cut salt-and-pepper hair, blow-dried into a short and smooth ducktail. She used just enough neutral-toned makeup to remind her business colleagues that no matter how capable, she was still a woman.

The real Bertha was no comparison to the off-putting figure of Joelle's imaginings. In fact, this Bertha seemed to be a real human, if a bit colorful. Her hair had been dyed a brilliant orange, reminding Joelle of an October sunset of such an intense hue that one couldn't bear to stare at it for long. Bertha's hair was set in a short, wash-and-dry frizzy permanent. Thin but prominent eyebrows were drawn over hairless flesh in a shade of pencil that had probably been labeled "auburn" on the package, but had the effect of chestnut brown when applied. A generous coat of mint green eye shadow, along with thick false eyelashes, adorned the same hazel eyes that Dexter had apparently inherited from her. Neon pink frosted lipstick added even more color to the rainbow. Bertha's hefty frame was clad in a short-sleeved denim camp shirt with a playing card, lottery ticket, and dice motif on the front, buttoned by large red rhinestones. Plastic earrings that mimicked bingo cards hung from her ears, nearly touching her shoulders.

Shocked by such a contrast between the imagined and the real Bertha, Joelle thought only to utter, "Nice shirt."

"You like it?" Bertha looked down at it, smiling as she inspected the motif. "I got it on sale at Wal-Mart. Only seven dollars." She lifted her forefinger in the air as though she had just thought of the most marvelous idea. "You know, I think if I get there by early tomorrow, I might be able to get you one, too. They looked like they had some really tiny sizes like you'd wear. But I can't promise. The rack was pretty picked over yesterday."

"Thanks for such a kind offer, but I'd never want you to go to so much trouble."

"I don't mind —"

"It's so sweet of you to offer," Joelle said, and she meant it.

"It's no trouble."

She smiled and shook her head. "Thanks, anyway." Joelle turned her attention to the road. *Why am I not surprised to see Bertha?*

"Hope you don't mind that I came along for the ride," she said, as if she were able to read Joelle's thoughts.

"Not at all." Joelle's response was more a result of reflexive manners than sincerity. "I had no idea you're a fan of classical music."

"Oh, I usually listen to country, but I'm always up for something wild and adventurous."

Joelle couldn't help but chuckle. She looked over at Dexter and wondered why he hadn't spoken since he left her front porch. Perhaps saying something cute might bring him out of what seemed to be a sour mood. "So, Dexter," she ventured, "your ad says you're cerebral. Why don't you say something smart?" Tilting her head, she threw him her best teasing grin.

"Something smart."

Bertha laughed and Joelle joined her. "I should have seen that one coming."

Dexter's lips refused to curl upward. "I take it Mother didn't tell you she was the one who wrote the ad."

Joelle froze. This wasn't good news.

"If you're looking to define 'cerebral' by

me, I'd say it means 'hasn't played a sport since high school.' " He cut his gaze to her just long enough to measure her reaction. "So if you're a member of Mensa, then you might not be too happy with me."

"What's Mensa?" Bertha wanted to know.

"It's a society for people who do very well on IQ tests," Dexter explained. "Very, very well."

"Oh." Bertha tittered uneasily.

"I doubt Mensa would have me," Joelle assured. Not eager to continue their conversation in its present vein, she was thankful to see the exit for the concert site. That was one of the longest miles Joelle could remember traveling.

Tension eased as absorption in the tasks of securing a parking place and a spot of grass to place their lawn chairs brought them together in a team effort, at least for a time. Joelle soon found herself sitting between Dexter and Bertha. Bertha continued to chat, even through the music. Dexter seemed to sulk.

After a couple of numbers, Joelle leaned toward her male companion and said in a low voice, "Was your mother lying when she said you like classical music?"

He shook his head.

"Then why do you act like you're headed

for the gas chamber?" she hissed.

Bertha interrupted before he could answer. "Are you two ready for supper? I sure am." Not waiting for a response, she placed the basket on her ample thighs and withdrew three lunch bags, passing two to Joelle and Dexter.

It wasn't until she had the brown paper bag in hand that Joelle realized her usual dinner hour was long past and she was more than ready to eat. Though unpromising on the outside, the package contained pleasant culinary surprises. Joelle discovered a roast beef sandwich. The oversized sesame seed bun was piled high with meat cooked rare and seasoned with lettuce, tomato, cheddar cheese, and horseradish sauce. As if that weren't enough, a large navel orange, a container of premium strawberry yogurt, a bag of chips, and a bar of imported chocolate followed.

"Wow, Bertha. This is more than I eat in two days."

"No wonder you're so tiny." Bertha waved a dismissive hand. "It won't hurt you to enjoy a decent meal now and then." Reaching again into the basket, Bertha handed each of them napkins, stainless steel spoons, and cans of soda.

"Mother," Dexter said, " 'decent' is not

always the same as 'large.' "

Joelle raised her eyebrows, surprised that Dexter had made an observation without prodding. All the same, she noticed he seemed to enjoy every last morsel of his supper, which was identical to hers.

During intermission, Joelle scraped the last of her yogurt out of its plastic container, deciding to save the orange, chips, and chocolate for another time. From the corner of her eye, she noticed a woman approach Dexter's chair and tap him on the shoulder.

From the other direction, Joelle heard Bertha say, "What is she doing here?"

CHAPTER 5

Dexter's eyes lit up for the first time that evening. "Anastasia! I thought you had to watch the kids tonight." He turned to one side and leaned toward the young woman. He rested his chin on his fist, obviously eager to hear her response.

"Genna didn't have to work after all. She and Jacob took the kids to a movie." Anastasia spoke with a thick accent. She squatted beside Dexter's chair, draping her left arm on top of its back.

Joelle couldn't help but notice Anastasia's fingernails were at least two inches in length. Each was lacquered sky blue. A tiny palm tree, leaves painted in green polish and trunk represented by bronze polish, had been meticulously painted on every nail. The effect was extraordinary, bringing to Joelle's mind tropical beaches. Though her reality was at present a cool night, Joelle could almost feel the sun's warmth mingling with a summer breeze. She wondered how long such artwork took to create.

At that moment, Bertha leaned over and said in a voice audible only to Joelle, "She's from one of those countries that used to be part of the Soviet Union. I don't know which one. I can't keep up with everything going on over there. Anyway, she's what they call an *au pair.* I think that's a fancy name for 'foreign baby-sitter for rich people.' "

"She seems awfully young for so much responsibility," Joelle whispered. "Barely out of her teens."

"I'd guess the same thing. Don't you think she's much too young for Dexter?"

Joelle hesitated. "I'm not sure that's for me to speculate."

"I know you're just being kind, dear, but you can feel free to speak your mind with me."

As much as Joelle wanted to console Bertha, she had a feeling anything she said would be repeated to Dexter, so she hesitated.

Bertha didn't wait for a response. "I must admit, I give you points for discretion. It's very ladylike of you not to badmouth your competition." Bertha patted Joelle on the knee. "You've been so good for Dexter."

Joelle's eyebrows shot up before she could contain her surprise. Dexter hadn't paid more than the most obligatory attention to her the whole evening. She couldn't imagine why Bertha would think she had had any effect on him at all.

"I hope you can encourage him to stay away from that little girl. If you want to know the truth, I'm afraid her main interest in my son is his American citizenship. What if she manages to get him to marry her so she can say she belongs here, too? And if he is fool enough to make it legal, how much do you want to bet she'll drop him like a hot potato? Probably before the ink dries on the wedding license. I'd hate to see him taken advantage of like that." Bertha tilted her head closer. "He needs a woman. Someone like you. I really mean it when I say I hope you'll see more of each other in the future."

Joelle stole a glance at Dexter and Anastasia. She was chattering in broken English about nothing, yet he never took his gaze away from her. Not that Joelle could blame him. With rich chestnut hair and smooth skin, Anastasia was attractive enough to entice any man. She had definitely bewitched Dexter.

Don't count on me seeing Dexter again

66

anytime soon.

Joelle sighed. Even if Dexter had entertained an interest in her, there hadn't been enough sparks to encourage Joelle to cultivate anything further. Looking over at Bertha as the last musical notes of Debussy's *Le Mer* floated through the cool night air, Joelle couldn't help but feel sorry for her. Dexter's mother was kind and concerned, albeit interfering. Silently she lifted the older woman's name to the Lord, praying that Bertha could find it in her heart to love the woman He one day planned for Dexter to marry, whether that woman were Anastasia or someone else. She added a request for her date, praying that Anastasia's interest wasn't mercenary but sincere.

The concert ended, and Dexter bade farewell to Anastasia without so much as introducing her to Joelle. As they rode home in silence, Joelle wondered if his oversight was a natural extension of his awkward manners, an admission that he had no interest in Joelle, or fear that Anastasia would become jealous. Not that it mattered. After this night, Joelle knew she'd never see any of them again.

Dexter parked in front of Joelle's house, got out of the car, and walked her to the door. After his indifference, she was surprised he made the effort. Even as she paused to say good night, Joelle sensed Bertha peering from the car, no doubt reading more into the gesture than Dexter intended.

"Thanks for the concert and picnic dinner, Dexter," Joelle managed, though she was eager to escape into the security of her house.

"Sure. But I can't take credit for the dinner. Or even the date, for that matter. Mother was the one with the concert tickets. I just went along for the ride."

"Then thank your mom again for me." She extended a smile she knew was bittersweet.

"Wait."

Joelle paused, surprised that Dexter had anything more to say to her.

"About tonight." He looked down at the porch and shuffled his feet, reminding her of a maladroit adolescent.

She struggled to rescue him from embarrassment. "No need to explain anything. I enjoyed the concert."

"I know, but I'm sorry my mother dragged you into the middle of all this. I mean, you seem like a nice person. She had no right to involve you in all this, especially since she knows about Anastasia."

"So you really are more than friends?"

"I hope so. I just wish Mother liked her. She just doesn't see Anastasia the way I do," he muttered without looking up.

"She's only trying to do what's best for you."

"In her way, I guess that's so." Dexter's eyes met Joelle's, narrowed in determination. "But if she doesn't like my choice of women, that's her problem, not mine. Or yours."

Joelle leaned against the front door. "But do you know why she doesn't like Anastasia?"

"She thinks she's too young." He hesitated as though he were thinking of other possibilities. "That's all I know."

"She's also worried because Anastasia is a foreigner and she might want to use you to gain U.S. citizenship."

"That's ridiculous."

"Perhaps it is. If I were you, I'd make sure before I did anything drastic." She looked him squarely in the face. "Normally I wouldn't give advice to someone I just met; but like you said, I got dragged into this, and sometimes wise counsel is easier to take from a stranger."

"Maybe so." He took on a thoughtful expression. "I'll remember what you said.

Thanks, Joelle."

As she watched Dexter walk back to the car, a thought suddenly occurred to her. *Lord, maybe this date was part of Your will after all.*

Dean could hardly concentrate on the lesson Fiona was giving for Singles' Night. Not that he needed to. He'd already heard about Jesus' weeping over the death of Lazarus in many previous Bible lessons. The brother of Martha and Mary, Lazarus had obviously been special to Jesus. Dean wondered what Lazarus had done to endear himself so much to the Lord to cause Him to cry over his death. As far as he could see, the Bible offered no clues. But who can explain friendship? Not just a relationship forged over common interests and goals, but a life-sustaining connection that transcends circumstances. Dean had enjoyed only two such friendships. One was with a high school pal who had joined the military just after graduation. Through E-mail, the occasional phone call, and infrequent visits, Dean managed to keep in touch with him no matter where in the world he was stationed.

The other friendship was with Joelle. Even now, when he was determined to stay mad at her, he couldn't. He tried not to stare across the room at her, even though he knew she was sitting so far away only because she had been ten minutes late. If she'd been sitting beside him, avoiding eye contact would have been easy. He couldn't look her way. Otherwise, she'd know all was forgiven before she could even apologize. And he had made up his mind that she would apologize for going against his advice, even if the wretched date hadn't interfered with Singles' Night. Surely she had learned her lesson by now. She would admit it. He wouldn't forgive her until she did.

A catch formed in his throat at a disturbing thought. *What if she hasn't learned her lesson? What if the date was so fantastic she's made a second one? What if Joelle fell for this guy she met through a personal ad?* The thought was too chilling to contemplate. He stared at his Bible, determined to put such ideas out of his mind.

"Good lesson, huh, Dean?" Nicole asked as everyone's Bibles closed.

He didn't want to admit he'd tuned out the lesson long ago. "Um, sure."

Nicole's hand gently touched his shoulder. "This is such a great group of friends here. Aren't we all lucky to have each other?"

Dean nodded, wondering why she felt the

need to make such an inane comment. He didn't have time to ponder her motives before Fiona, who was also in charge of the night's entertainment, announced the game.

"Is everybody up for Twister?" An enthusiastic smile covered her face.

A round of applause and a couple of whistles greeted the suggestion.

"At least this game doesn't involve sports questions." Dean hadn't expected Joelle to sneak up on him. He gasped in surprise. Her hot breath tickled his ear when she whispered. The breezy scent of her breath mints, mingled with her trademark perfume, wafted to his nostrils.

Dean's heart betrayed him by lurching. "Lucky for you," he managed.

She wrinkled her nose. "Although it does require one to be very agile." Joelle gave him a good-natured poke in the ribs.

Dean wasn't able to respond before he was summoned to help spread out the thin plastic sheet decorated with colored dots. He didn't relish the idea of contorting himself so he could place his hands and feet on the different dots at the whim of a spinning wheel. But to be a good sport, he had to go along.

After only a few spins of the wheel, the singles found themselves in a tangled mess.

Dean was positioned with his left hand on the same spot as Joelle's. In turn, she had wiggled into a stance that placed her partially on top of him. He knew it wouldn't take much for him to lose his equilibrium, but Dean was determined to stay upright — or at least as upright as he could, considering he was balanced on all fours.

Despite his efforts, the next spin proved fatal. As Dean tried to move his right foot to a blue dot, he dropped to the floor, twisting and landing on his back. His flying limbs nudged Joelle, who fell on top of him.

For a split second, her face was inches away from his. Her teal green eyes were filled with astonishment, her pink lips parted. He had a sudden impulse to kiss her. He wondered what everyone else would think, should he make such a bold move. He imagined they would first stand and gawk. Then, Zach would start the applause. Fiona, Nicole, and Ashlynn would follow. Zach would whistle lewdly enough to embarrass Joelle, but all in good fun. As Dean fantasized about their reaction, a voice interrupted.

"You lose, Dean!" Nicole stood over him. Her eyes, rimmed heavily by black eyeliner, sparkled victoriously. Her mouth, glazed in a bold red, was contorted into a smirk.

The applause in Dean's imagination ceased.

"You lose, too, Joelle," Nicole added.

"Oh, all right," Joelle conceded, slipping away from Dean's grasp.

He hopped up in one fluid motion, hoping his nonchalant motion would belie his fantasies. "You okay, Joelle?"

As she nodded, he led her to a sofa that had been a castoff from a church member. "So are we still on for our coffee?" she asked as she sat beside him on the green-and-brown-plaid couch.

Suddenly he remembered once again that he was supposed to be mad. He decided to play it coy. "I had no idea you were still interested."

Her blond eyebrows shot up. "Who says I'm not interested?"

"I don't know." He shrugged. "I thought maybe I'd be old news after your hot date." Dean shot her a look from the corner of his eye. "You did go out on another date, didn't you?"

"Unfortunately, I did."

He brightened at the word "unfortunately," even though he was disappointed by the confirmation that she had disregarded his advice. "At least you didn't let it interfere with tonight. Everyone would have missed you," he hastened to add, lest she realize he was the one who would have missed her the most.

"I suppose." A series of hoots indicated that Fiona had fallen victim to an inability to wrench herself into an odd shape. After the momentary distraction, Joelle's hand rested on his knee. "So are we still on for coffee or not?"

"Sure, but only if you promise to tell me all about this awful date of yours."

"Promise."

The rest of the meeting flew by, with Dean even managing to emerge the winner of one of the games. After the closing prayer, everyone headed to the parking lot. Dean was sorry he hadn't arranged to pick Joelle up and take her to the meeting. He would miss her presence in his car. Dean let out a sigh as they made their way to separate vehicles. Without warning, someone touched his shoulder. He turned his head and spotted Nicole.

"Going home alone, Dean?"

"After coffee, yes."

Nicole tilted her head as though she were waiting for him to offer her an invitation to join him. When she saw none was forthcoming, she uttered, "Too bad." Flashing him a smile, she waved and headed toward her red Mustang Cobra.

Dean felt a moment of guilt. In an effort to be sure he and Joelle were alone for coffee, he had let his manners fly out the window. Well, maybe Nicole could tag along next time.

As agreed, Joelle followed Dean's car to a favorite drive-in restaurant on Route 81. When Dean had suggested they take advantage of the comfortable spring night, she readily acquiesced. Lingering in the brisk night air at a picnic table sounded good, especially when dessert promised to be a large hot fudge brownie sundae with zebra ice cream, walnuts, whipped cream, and a cherry. The prospect was enough to justify a drive several miles over crooked rural roads past the county line.

Yet as she watched Dean's taillights, hot fudge sundaes were the last thing on Joelle's mind. She had seen Nicole talking to him as they left the church. Joelle hadn't liked the flirtatious look the other woman had cast Dean's way as she waved good-bye. In fact, Joelle hadn't liked anything Nicole had done all night. She had stayed by Dean constantly, talking to him every chance she got. Joelle didn't know Nicole well, but she was aware of Nicole's reputation as a vixen.

After the evening's performance, she could see why. Even from across the room, Nicole's seductive body language was all too easy to read. So masterfully did she play the role that Joelle was surprised Nicole bothered to associate herself with any church. Even so, someone as sweet as Dean had no business anywhere near Nicole. Surely he had no experience with such a calculating temptress. She had to alert Dean. Doing so was only her duty.

She pulled in to the drive-in restaurant right behind Dean, gravel crackling in protest under tires. Jumping out of the car without bothering to lock the door, Joelle hurried across the sidewalk to Dean's side. She didn't bother with subtleties. "So what did Nicole have to say?"

The grin faded from his face as he continued to walk toward the substantial line of customers under the bright fluorescent lights. "Have to say about what?"

"Don't pull that innocent act with me. I saw her flirting with you all night, and then she was talking to you while we were leaving." Her voice took on an edge that astonished even her. Looking for a distraction, she swatted a few bugs that were flying near her face, attracted to the sweet smells of her perfume and hair spray.

"Maybe I'm acting innocent because I have nothing to hide," Dean protested. Lifting his head slightly, he arched one auburn eyebrow. "If I didn't know you better, Joelle, I'd think you were jealous."

"Jealous?" Joelle stopped in her tracks, right in front of the entrance. Her mouth dropped open in objection. "What a typical male you are, Dean Nichols! Conceited as all get-out." Balling her hand into a fist, she tapped him on his forearm just hard enough to emphasize her point.

"I'm surprised at you. I didn't think you were a female chauvinist, Joelle Jamison."

Joelle stepped to one side, allowing a couple of the other customers to leave the line without scraping cones of chocolate-dipped ice cream against her sleeve. However, she didn't let them stop her from making her point. She narrowed her eyes and set her lips in a straight line. "I don't have to be a female chauvinist to see a shark on the attack."

He flashed a wide, wolflike smile. "All the more reason for you to stay away from the male sharks you meet through the personals, my dear."

"Male sharks!" she hissed. Bowing her head, Joelle dug the toe of her ballet flat into dust-covered gravel.

This was not the moment to let Dean know she had already looked through the personals and chosen another date.

CHAPTER 6

Do you enjoy elegant evenings? Days at the ballpark? Afternoons at the theater? Walks in the rain? So do I! Are you 25–30 and believe variety is the spice of life? Do you want to share your spicy life with a devoted Christian man? Then give me a call today!

Intrigued, Joelle had done just that. A man named Wilbert Webster had answered the phone. After ascertaining that Wilbert had placed the ad himself and that he really wanted to meet Christian women, Joelle breathed an inward sigh of relief.

Wilbert wasn't shy about presenting his potential date with questions of his own. Not surprisingly, he asked about her Christian walk first. Nervous, Joelle had to admit she was still a new Christian. She was relieved when he answered that every Christian was new at the start, and he didn't mind. He seemed impressed by the physical description she offered upon his request, even though Joelle was careful not to exaggerate her best features. When they discovered a mutual fascination with old movies and travel, Joelle could feel his interest growing.

"I hope you don't mind spending an evening with a computer geek." Wilbert's smooth, mellow voice would have been at home on radio airwaves. Computer geek or not, Joelle thought she'd enjoy listening to him talk about anything *ad infinitum,* even if the term did force an image in her mind of a scrawny fellow with thick glasses and a pocket protector. "At least," Wilbert continued, "that's what my friends like to call me, since I repair computers for a living."

"Oh, they're just jealous," she answered.

"I'll have to tell them you said that." The tone of his voice told her he spoke in jest.

"Just don't give them my real name or address," she quipped.

"Don't worry. I'll protect you. None of them can bench press as much weight as I can."

The image of a scrawny guy faded, replaced in Joelle's mind by a heavyset man with bulging biceps and chest muscles. "I admit, I'm impressed."

"Don't be. I can't lift all that much. And just so you won't be disappointed when you meet me in person, I don't look anything like those guys on pro wrestling."

"Thank goodness!" She laughed.

"I don't have that much time to spend at the gym," he said without apology. "But I do spend a lot of time at church, especially since we sponsor a Christian school. I maintain the church and school computers. I teach advanced computer courses."

"So you're a teacher, too?"

"Not professional. The course is an elective for juniors and seniors, and I teach on my lunch hour. If you're wondering how I manage that, I have to thank my company. They're pretty progressive. My boss lets me take a little extra time each day so I can be free to give back to the community." He let out a little chuckle. "I work more than enough hours to make up for the time, though."

Joelle couldn't help but be impressed. Not even Dean could argue against someone with such dedication to church and community. When the conversation wound down to a close, Joelle felt at ease planning a date for the following Friday night.

"Just one thing," she asked as they bid farewell.

"What's that?"

"Do you promise not to bring your mother along?"

"My mother?" His voice inflected with surprise. "What would she be doing on our date?"

"Trust me, you don't want to know the details."

He chuckled. "Sounds like you've been through this before."

"Just twice."

"Me, too. Maybe the third time's a charm."

The appliance store was devoid of customers, a fact that surprised Dean since Friday afternoons were usually boons for retail businesses. Scanning the small showroom of thirty or so appliances displayed in tight formation, Dean didn't see the owner. He ventured to the back of the store, finding the cubbyhole that Earl used as a business office. Dean knocked on the door. "Earl? Are you there?"

A man in his midfifties emerged. "Dean! Good to see you . . . except I bet this means the old washer finally died?" Behind Earl's jovial demeanor was a note of sympathy.

Dean answered with a weak nod. Whenever events in his personal life and business tried his patience, Dean drew strength from the verses in scripture on pride. His favorite was 1 John 2:16: "For all that is in the world, the lust of the flesh, and the lust of the eyes, and the pride of life, is not of the Father, but is of the world."

Even with this verse in mind, Dean cringed as he followed Earl to the counter. The retailer didn't bother with a sales pitch or show Dean any new washer models. Earl already knew just the machine Dean would be purchasing. Dean always did business with Earl, and the appliance salesman was cognizant that Wash 'n Wear was barely turning a profit. He would have to ask Earl to extend more credit if the new machine was to be delivered anytime soon. Even then, "soon" was a relative concept when the time to order a commercial machine arrived. Since Earl didn't keep heavy-duty machines fitted with coin slots in stock, he would have to special order the washer. At least a month was sure to pass before the new machine would be delivered.

Dean tried not to let his discouragement show. With money a scarce commodity, he had delayed the purchase of a new washer as long as he could. Three times, he had repaired the old machine as it sputtered to the end of its useful life. After three strikes,

Dean figured the point had come where sinking more cash into repairs would be folly.

Dean sighed. One day, after he had expanded his business to take in alterations and dry cleaning, he'd be able to pay cash on the barrel for any washer or dryer — even the top-of-the-line models. For now, he would have to swallow his worldly pride and beg Earl's indulgence.

He cleared his throat. "Earl, I hate to ask, but —"

The older man held up his hand, palm facing his customer. "Then don't." Earl put down his hand and began typing. Without looking away from the computer screen, he said, "Your credit's good with me."

Burden lifted, Dean felt so light he almost thought he could fly. "Thanks, Earl."

"No problem." He kept typing. "Besides, your account is paid up. I'd give you all the credit you need since you're a friend, not to mention you're on the finance committee at church. You're a good customer, too. I know you're as good as your word." He paused as a small machine beside the computer printed out a receipt.

Dean recalled the passage of scripture old Miss Williams had made her Sunday school class memorize when they were barely in high school. Her insistence on the verses in the fifth chapter of Matthew had been motivated partly by her belief in Bible memorization. It didn't help that she'd overheard Bobby Johnson taking the Lord's name in vain when he struck out at the church baseball game the previous Saturday.

Dean felt a smile tingle upon his lips. Miss Williams was certainly feasting with Jesus in heaven on this day. In the meantime, Bobby had long since relocated to New York City and become successful on Wall Street, the last Dean had heard.

No matter. The scriptural admonition had remained with him all these years:

> But I say unto you, Swear not at all; neither by heaven; for it is God's throne: nor by the earth; for it is his footstool: neither by Jerusalem; for it is the city of the great King. Neither shalt thou swear by thy head, because thou canst not make one hair white or black. But let your communication be, Yea, yea; Nay, nay: for whatsoever is more than these cometh of evil.

Earl's easy voice, accented by his Southern upbringing, brought Dean back to the present. "Yep, you're one person whose word I'd trust any day. Can't say that about everybody these days, I'm afraid." He handed Dean the receipt. "Got anything to do tonight?"

"Not really . . . unless you think going home to microwave a hot dog and spend the night in front of the television is exciting."

"You've got something special to do now." Earl pulled a couple of tickets out of the pocket of his faded blue denim shirt and handed them to Dean. "My wife bought these a couple of months ago. Since then, her sister came down sick, and she had to go to Oklahoma to nurse her."

"I'm sorry."

"Thanks, but she'll be okay. So now I'm stuck with these tickets for a play I didn't want to see, nohow. I don't much hearken to theater stuff. Especially musicals." He wrinkled his nose. "To tell you the honest truth, I'm glad to get out of it."

Dean looked at the tickets. They granted entrance to the Bard Dinner Theater for a buffet and performance of *The Sound of Music.*

"Oh, and they feed you, too," Earl added.

"Are you sure you can't use these? You can always eat and run." Dean cracked a smile.

"Naw. I'd rather go bowling. Besides, who would I go with, an old married man like me? Now you go on and ask some pretty girl you know." Earl winked. "Women love them sappy stories, don't you think?"

"So I've heard." Dean grinned. "Thanks, Earl. I know just whom to ask."

On the night of the date, Joelle thought about how she was grateful Wilbert had suggested they take in a show at a dinner theater miles away. She had no desire to run into Dean while she was out with Wilbert. Even being seen by mutual friends would be risky. In their close-knit community, gossip traveled quickly. Not that she cared what Dean thought. Of course, he meant well to caution her against dating strange men. What else were friends for? But she just wasn't in the mood for any of his lectures or withering looks. Both were sure to be the result, should Dean discover she was out with Wilbert.

As Joelle searched her jewelry box for the pearl drop earrings she always wore with her little black dress, she recalled Dean's reaction to her story of her date with Dexter. Or rather, her date with Bertha. When Dean chuckled and pointed out how wise Joelle had been to win over Dexter's mother, she knew all was forgiven. Still, she wasn't sure he'd be so charitable, should he discover she had made yet another date with a stranger.

"Why can't I seem to stop worrying about Dean?" she asked her reflection as she struggled to slide the earring-back to the right place on the post. An angry-looking young woman stared back, hair deliberately mussed and sticking out in a questionable fashion, eyebrows curved disagreeably, eyes narrowed into slits, and her mouth a pink slash. "Dean Nichols has no hold over me. He has no right to tell me who to see and who not to see."

So why am I hiding?

Frustrated, she dropped the earring back and heard it bounce and roll across the hardwood floor until it landed somewhere underneath her dresser. With an exclamation of distress, she knelt in front of the furniture, peering underneath until she eyed the little piece of gold lying in the far corner, amidst dust unreachable by even her best efforts with a vacuum. Wrinkling her nose, she lay on her stomach and stretched her arm and fingers to their fullest extent. The piece of metal was just within reach of her middle finger. With a little grunt, she slid it toward her. Successful in its retrieval, she blew off the dust it had accumulated on its journey and rose to her feet.

The abrupt motion made her realize she had developed a dull headache. Fighting pain was the last thing she needed to worry about tonight. After glancing one last time in the mirror to determine she was satisfied enough with her appearance, Joelle headed for the kitchen and the aspirin her mom kept on a spinning rack in the cabinet.

"You look absolutely lovely, Joelle," her mom noticed.

"Thanks." Joelle reached into the refrigerator for the milk. She poured herself a small glass and retrieved a little plastic bottle with a yellow label from the cabinet.

"What's the matter? Why are you taking aspirin?"

"Headache," she explained before swallowing the tablets.

"What are you doing with a headache? You're not that nervous about this date, are you?"

She shook her head. "I don't know why my head hurts."

"Maybe it's stress."

"I hadn't thought of that." Joelle's head pounded even more, and she noticed the pain had traveled to the back of her neck.

With her left hand, she leaned against the kitchen counter. She clutched the throbbing muscle with her right hand and tried to massage away the ache.

Her mother came up behind her. With her fingers on Joelle's shoulders, she placed one thumb on each side of the base of her neck and pressed several times.

"Thanks. That feels better."

"No doubt. I can feel the tension in your muscles. Poor thing." She kept up the pressure on Joelle's neck. "You certainly have no reason to be nervous. Whoever this Wilbert guy is, he'd be crazy not to be thrilled with you, both inside and out."

"Thanks, Mom. You always know what to say."

"What else are mothers for?" She patted Joelle's back, ending the therapeutic rub. Leaning against the counter she had just wiped down, Mom folded her arms and took on a knowing expression that reminded Joelle of the Mona Lisa. "You've really been dining on a feast of men lately, haven't you?"

"A feast of men? Mom!" Joelle set her empty glass in the sink. "What's that supposed to mean?"

"Nothing." Eleanor's narrow shoulders rose in a shrug. "It's just that since you've been working at the doctor's office, you hadn't met all that many men. Now, all of a sudden, you seem to be going out with a different guy every week."

Joelle didn't remember a time when she was more grateful to hear the doorbell ring.

"Your dad's still out. Want me to get that?"

"That's okay, thanks." Joelle shook her head. "If he's worth meeting, I'll make sure to introduce you."

When Joelle opened the door, she was shocked to find a man standing on the porch wearing stained blue jeans and a faded gray T-shirt that looked as though it had seen a year of workouts at the gym. She felt her eyes widen, but soon composed her features into a poker face.

"Wow!" His mouth flew open.

"Uh, thanks, I guess." An idea occurred to Joelle as she remembered job seekers from the previous week. "Look, if you're canvassing the neighborhood looking to do chores, I'm sorry. We don't have anything for you."

He shook his head so hard, a few brown curls fell out of place. A quick run-through with his hand replaced them well enough. "I'm Wilbert. I'm here for Joelle. I'm assuming that's you?"

"You assume right." Despite her best efforts, Joelle's eyes scanned the rough-hewn man before her. Her tone of voice betrayed her disappointment. "But —"

"I know what you're going to say. Didn't I promise an elegant evening at the dinner theater?" He nodded. "That's right. I did, and I still plan to keep my promise. I even have my suit in the car." He cocked his head toward a late-model red sports car parked in front of the house. "It's just that I forgot I need to do something else first."

"Um, should I ask what that something else is?"

"I promised I'd clean up the churchyard after work today. It's got to look nice by Sunday."

"But it's only Friday."

"I know, but I have classes all day tomorrow. I'm working on my degree."

"Oh." Since her own mother was pursuing her education, Joelle understood all too well how lessons could interfere with someone's personal life.

"I wish I'd thought to call before you got dressed, but you wouldn't mind helping me, would you? The school has showers in the gym locker rooms. You can change there, and then we can go right to the show. The janitor and his wife will be there, so you don't need to worry."

She consulted her watch. "But won't we

miss the play?"

"We can see the second show. The tickets are good for either one, as long as we go tonight."

Joelle shrugged. "All right. I guess a little hard work never hurt anybody."

His face lit up with a smile. "Thanks. I really appreciate it."

As she changed in her bedroom, Joelle wondered if Wilbert were putting her through some kind of test and what other women would have done in her place. Sighing, she thought about Dean. No way would he ever pull a stunt like that on any woman.

Dean. I wonder what he's doing tonight. Suddenly she became aware that her headache, which she thought had subsided, had returned to make her head pound. She resolved to take a second dose of aspirin as soon as she could.

Folding her dress, which was thankfully a knit that wouldn't wrinkle, she placed the garment in an overnight bag. Black hose, pearl earrings, bracelet, and necklace followed. Pulling a red T-shirt over her head, Joelle realized that getting dressed and redressed would result in her hair transforming from deliberately messy to really and truly messy. She decided to toss in the hair wax, a comb, and a can of superhold spray. Then, remembering that a school locker room wouldn't necessarily provide soap, she added shampoo, soap, a towel, and a blow dryer. Last, but not least, followed the aspirin.

The overnight bag was bulging by the time she had finished packing. "Everything but the kitchen sink." She shook her head.

As she reemerged to the living room, Joelle cast her mom a grateful look for keeping Wilbert occupied while she changed. Her mom's response was to wink, a sure sign she wasn't too certain she liked hardworking Wilbert. Joelle sighed inwardly. She could count on a heart-to-heart when she returned home that night.

"See you later, Mom."

"When will you be home?"

"We should be home by midnight," Wilbert promised as the phone started to ring.

Joelle wondered if she should stay to see if the call was for her, but Eleanor shooed her out. "I'll get that. You don't have any time to lose. If it's for you, I'll take a message."

She could feel her mother's eyes on them as they walked to Wilbert's car. Wilbert did pause at the passenger side and open Joelle's door, a definite plus. *Maybe there are some men other than Dean who remember what chivalry is, after all!*

CHAPTER 7

"By the way, Joelle, I need to stop by the dry cleaners," Wilbert said as they approached the next town. "I hope you don't mind."

"Sure. I understand." Joelle forced herself to smile. How many more delays did he plan to propose?

He pulled the car into a small parking lot in front of the cleaners and tilted his head toward the backseat. Following his direction, Joelle saw a large, lumpy duffel bag. "Mind taking those in for me?"

"Um, sure. As long as I don't have to pay the bill," she quipped.

"Maybe next time." Wilbert chuckled.

Although taken aback by his odd request, Joelle accomplished the errand quickly and soon slid back into the passenger seat.

"Thanks." He flashed a smile. "Oh, and by the way, I have to stop by my apartment. I just realized I forgot my good clothes. But before that, I need to stop at the gas station."

"We're getting a lot done this evening," she remarked, somehow managing to keep the edge of irritation off her voice. "You don't need to stop for a haircut, too, do you?"

"That won't happen until our second date." His serious expression made her wonder if he really was joking. "Although I just remembered I do need to pick up a quart of milk at the grocery store."

As hard as she tried to be patient, Joelle couldn't help but stew as she sat in the car, sweating from the heat, as he made one stop after another. "I'm beginning to wonder if you even have tickets for the play," she noted a half hour later as they parked in the lot of a six-unit apartment building. "Maybe you really don't and are just stalling until we run out of time." She let out a strained giggle.

He snapped his fingers. "Oh, I'm glad you reminded me. I've got to get those out of my sock drawer."

Joelle didn't answer. Her capacity to be amused by the absentminded professor type had surpassed its limit.

Wilbert hopped out of the car. Before he shut the door, he turned to Joelle and leaned his head inside. "Aren't you coming with me?"

"You mean, into your apartment? Alone?" She let her voice drift off so he could guess the source of her protests. Certainly she wouldn't need to spell them out.

Wilbert bristled so he stood fully upright. "I'm not going to attack you, if that's what you're afraid of. Anyway, both of my roommates are home. If I try anything, you can tell them to beat me up."

Upset that she had offended her date, Joelle acquiesced by exiting her side of the car. Wilbert had given her no indication he couldn't be trusted. Still, she made a mental note to bolt if she saw no evidence of his roommates.

Her anxiety proved unfounded. As soon as they entered, Joelle saw two young men who looked to be in their early twenties situated in front of the television. The sounds emanating from the oversized box were angry. Curious, Joelle turned her attention to the show. Overdeveloped men shouted each other down, vowing revenge against one another. A bikini-clad woman with long hair and muscular arms added screaming remarks. A slightly smaller man, dressed in a referee's uniform, acted as though he wanted the shouting to stop. Since his protests were weak, Joelle wasn't convinced.

"What's the matter?" one of the guys asked. "Haven't you seen pro wrestling before?"

"Apparently not," Joelle answered. She looked at her inquisitor, only to find his face was hidden by the brim of a Yankees' baseball cap.

The second roommate took a swig of beer from a brown bottle. "Have a seat and take a look, then."

"She doesn't have time," Wilbert answered. "Joelle, as you can see, this place is a mess. Bert and Josh don't seem to mind, but I'd sure appreciate it if you could pick up a little while I get my things together. You don't mind, do you?"

Joelle had been too absorbed by the television program to notice the room until Wilbert mentioned it. Looking around, she could see the place was, indeed, a mess. Five pizza cartons that appeared to be a week old were positioned in different places on the floor. Empty beer bottles and soda cans occupied various places on mismatched end tables, sofa arms, and the floor. Some had landed as though their consumers attempted to pitch them inside an overflowing black plastic trash can and missed their target by anywhere from a few inches to several feet.

Balled-up wads of paper decorated the room like so much confetti. A stack of newspapers, magazines, and mail had become so large that the highest pieces had toppled out of position, resulting in a mishmash of paper. For Wilbert's sake, Joelle hoped no bills that needed to be paid anytime soon were hidden in the pile. Suddenly, she noticed the room was permeated with a stench that reminded her of how a dirty gym would smell if a pizza parlor were operating in the middle of it.

"Um —" was all she could manage before she realized Wilbert had left the room.

Baseball Cap laughed. "He's long gone, honey. You'd better get crackin' if you expect to go anywhere else tonight."

The other roommate let out a hearty burp. "Why don't you go in the kitchen and do the dishes? The dishwasher's broken, but there's plenty of detergent to do them by hand."

"I didn't come here to do the dishes." Joelle folded her arms.

"Suit yourself. But like I said, he'll stall until at least some of this work is done." Baseball Cap shrugged. "He does this to everybody he brings here."

"He does?"

"Yeah. See, we don't mind the mess. He

does, but he doesn't want to pick up after us on principle."

"In that case, neither do I." Determined not to involve herself in their feud, Joelle plopped onto a chair. Only after she felt moisture on the side of her thigh did she jump back up. The culprit turned out to be a discarded half-eaten piece of pizza, with pepperoni and bits of cheese and ground beef still clinging to a sea of tomato sauce. The food had been wedged between the cushion and arm. Joelle didn't want to venture a guess as to how long ago.

"Sorry about that," Baseball Cap commented.

Without replying, Joelle headed into the small kitchen in search of a paper towel. Perhaps if she got a little water on the spot right away, there would be some hope of getting out the red paste and yellow grease in the laundry.

Not surprisingly, the kitchen table was piled with junk. Books and papers occupied the seats of the matching chairs. Sighing, Joelle headed for the counters. Behind a stack of open cookie containers and several boxes of cereal, she discovered a paper towel rack. To her amazement, the rack housed a clean, new roll. Noticing a pattern of blue and pink bears, she expected the bachelors hadn't noticed the motif was meant for a nursery. But she wasn't complaining. Finally she maneuvered the faucet around a sink of dirty dishes and dampened the towel. With a little scrubbing, Joelle cleared most of the spot from her jeans.

Task completed, she located another overflowing trash can. This one was surrounded by paper grocery bags filled with more garbage. Joelle tossed the crumpled towel in the general direction of the mess. Her reward was to see it land in one of the bags. Though her basketball skills were lacking, the sheer number of bags had guaranteed her two points. She returned to the living room, where she hoped to find Wilbert. He still hadn't emerged from his room.

"I know it's none of my business," she offered to Baseball Cap, "but cleaning up the old food you have lying around will do more to get rid of roaches than all that boric acid powder you have around the baseboards."

"Maybe. But they're permanent residents. They were part of the welcome wagon when we got here."

"Shh!" hissed the other guy. "I'm trying to hear the TV."

The program had switched from wrestling to a commercial featuring women wearing hot pants and halter tops. Between the disorder and the prurient programming, Joelle had had enough. "Tell Wilbert I've gone back to the car."

"Sure."

Joelle didn't believe they'd tell him anything, but at that point, being alone in a sweltering vehicle seemed better than enduring another moment in Wilbert's apartment.

"Too bad," she heard one of the men observe as she swung the door shut behind her. "She looked better than most of the others."

A grin touched Joelle's lips in spite of herself. No way was she returning to such a disaster. As she waited for Wilbert, Joelle opted to mill around the common area and enjoy what little breeze the day offered.

Her date snuck up on her moments later as she observed two young sisters playing in a small sandbox. "I thought I told you to help out in the house. What are you doing out here?"

"Waiting for you. Ready to go?" Joelle made sure her tone didn't invite further inquiry or criticism.

Without another word, he led her to the car. Joelle broke the silence as they pulled back into traffic. "What's the deal with your roommates? If you can't stand a mess, why don't you either hire a maid or throw them out?"

"One, I can't afford a maid. Two, they're my brothers. They're both still in school and don't have anywhere else to go. Don't ask for details. Besides, it looks to me like any nice girl wouldn't mind helping out a little. None of the others seemed to mind."

"Then where are they?" She regretted her retort as soon as it left her lips. "I'm sorry. Look, I can understand not wanting to leave your brothers in the lurch, but as long as it's your apartment, why can't you make them pick up?"

"I've tried. Believe me."

"You could at least put your foot down about the beer drinking."

"What they do is their business." His eyes narrowed. "I don't need criticism from you or anyone else."

Joelle and Wilbert rode in silence. Despite his defense of them, she wondered why Wilbert let his brothers get away with drinking beer all day and treating his home like a dump. And to think — he expected her to clean it! Just like he expected her to clean his churchyard. She started to confront him about that issue when she noticed his mouth was clamped shut. At that moment she decided to remain mute.

I agreed to help with the churchyard, and I won't go back on my promise now. If we see each other again, I can always bring up the subject later.

Joelle was glad when the church came into sight. The sanctuary building stood grandly in the center of a large plot of land, dominating the nearby landscape. A white steeple looked down upon huge oaks, sugar maples, and pines. The church building and the accompanying school, secluded among the trees, created a majestic picture.

Only the sign in front indicated strength and energy. It read:

King's Army Church and Christian School
Dr. Dillon Douglas, Pastor
Sunday's Sermon: How Does God Define Victory?

"This facility is really something, isn't it?" Wilbert asked as they exited his car.

Joelle continued her survey of the grounds. The colossal brick church building looked strong enough to withstand attacks. Rectangular sections protruding from the main portion of the building indicated at least ten classrooms. A well-maintained playground included a set of four swings, two slides, a tire swing, monkey bars, and a merry-go-round.

"This is quite nice," she readily agreed.

"We use the classrooms adjacent to the playground for Sunday school. During the week, they're used by the lower grades of the school."

Another building loomed to the left. "What's that?"

"The high school." Wilbert's pride was obvious. "We go from kindergarten all the way up through the twelfth grade. Almost five hundred students are enrolled here. Some drive fifty miles, one way, to go to this school."

"Wow!"

Still looking over the area, Joelle noticed a flat parcel of property with enough land to accommodate a soccer field and a baseball diamond. Two sets of bleachers were painted red and black. She could read "The King's Army" on the nearest scoreboard. The mascot — a knight in the armor of a Crusader — was painted on the board. He looked ready for battle.

"I'll say it again. You do have an impressive church and school facility." She gave Wilbert what she knew to be a hesitant look. "But there's only one thing. Do we have to finish working all this tonight?"

Wilbert chuckled. "Oh, no. I just promised

to get the church grounds into shape. The high school is sending someone else over tomorrow to take care of the sports fields and the rest of their campus."

Placing her hand over her heart and exhaling, Joelle didn't bother to conceal her relief. For Wilbert to change their plans at the last minute was one thing — after all, he did make a promise, and anyone could be forgiven for being a little disorganized occasionally. But there was no way the two of them would be able to manicure the land surrounding both the church and the school and still be able to make the play. Now maybe they had a chance. "Why don't I do the mowing?"

"Sorry, but I don't think that's a good idea. For one thing, all we have is a standard mower, not a riding one like we really need. To make things worse, it doesn't work well. It tends to cut off without notice. I can barely handle it myself."

"What do you want me to do, then? I enjoy planting flowers, although I don't suppose you have anything like that in mind."

"Not today. Sorry." He surveyed the area, then inclined his head toward a far corner of the churchyard. "How about whacking a few weeds? That area over there needs tend-ing. The tool's in the shed. I'll be right back."

Joelle looked at the area. She felt her mouth open in astonishment. Weeds at least three feet tall awaited. She turned back in his direction to protest, only to discover Wilbert had disappeared.

"Well, if that doesn't beat everything I've ever seen." Joelle placed her hands on her hips, not caring what strangers in passing cars might think. If she had brought her own car, Joelle would have been tempted to make a run for the vehicle, put the pedal to the metal, and make a fast getaway over winding roads to the calm of her house. But she was stuck.

Not seeing anything useful to do while she waited, Joelle sat in one of the swings. Slowly she rocked the swing back and forth, her feet barely leaving the ground. After a few minutes, Wilbert emerged from the tool shed. He was carrying a long wooden stick with a curved blade attached.

"Here you go." He held the instrument as if it were a prized possession.

She made a show of trying to locate an electrical cord. "Um, where do you plug this in?"

"You don't, silly. It runs on pure muscle." Wilbert observed what little portion of her biceps peered from under her short-sleeved shirt. "If you do this type of work often enough, your muscles will be hard as rocks." He handed her the outmoded instrument.

Joelle wanted to beg one more time to run the mower. Surely any gas-powered machine would be preferable to a blade and stick that looked like a nineteenth-century relic.

Before she could open her mouth, Wilbert wished her luck and headed for the waiting mower. Joelle knew argument would only delay the beginning of their real date. She refused to consider the work portion as part of the entertaining evening he had promised. Instead, she hoped to get the task done quickly and then make every effort to forget it. Whistling a series of tuneless notes, she headed for the corner. After assessing the best place to start, she whacked the far edge of the patch of prolific plants. On the third stroke, the blade flew off, sailing through the air as if it were a paper airplane instead of a piece of metal.

Grumbling, Joelle ventured into the overgrowth. Weeds scratched against her pants, making her glad she'd opted for jeans instead of shorts. After searching a few feet, she found the missing blade. She picked it up and pressed the sharp edged metal back onto the worn handle.

"There you go," she said to herself, pounding the metal an extra time for good measure. "Must not have been on very well to start with. Now I can get moving."

The next two strokes were successful, but to her frustration, the blade flew off again during the third swipe. Joelle could see this was a flaw that couldn't be corrected without attaching the blade to the handle with glue. Refusing to admit defeat, she established a pattern. Her best burst of energy went into the first whack, since the blade was properly in place at that point. On the second stroke, the edge would wiggle, allowing her to make less headway than with the first swipe. Before the third attempt, Joelle would reposition the blade before it had a chance to fall off. This process considerably inhibited her advancement.

She kept at it until Wilbert finally appeared behind her to say he was through mowing the churchyard. They were free to shower and go to the play.

"Nice job," Wilbert complimented her as he studied the corner. "I can't believe how much you've improved this area."

"Especially with a whacker that's falling apart." She studied the remaining weeds. "It still needs a lot of work."

He took the instrument from her willing

hands. Motioning for her to follow, he began to walk to the shed. "That's all right. No one else wants to bother with that corner. Too many rats, you know."

"Rats?" Joelle shuddered. "I wish you had said something earlier."

He shrugged. "I see you made out okay." After vanishing into the shed, he emerged again to lock the door. Wilbert took as much care in securing the outbuilding as Joelle imagined he would have in locking up a valuable treasure. Considering the state of the tools inside, Joelle wondered why he bothered. She decided not to make her observation known to her date.

Joelle relished the light breeze that cooled her as they made their way across the campus to the high school. The gym was locked, so Wilbert summoned the janitor to let them in.

"Nice weather today, huh, Wilbert?" the older man asked as he jangled several keys, searching for the right one.

"Sure is." Wilbert sent him an apologetic smile. "Sorry I had to bother you, Al."

"That's okay. Had to unlock it for the wife, anyhow. She'll be here in a minute to mop the gym floor."

After bidding Al a good day, Joelle slipped past the gray door marked GIRLS. "I'll be out in a few minutes."

He checked his watch. "Don't worry. We've got time."

All the same, Joelle did her best not to delay. She quickly showered and shampooed her hair. As warm water covered her body, its soothing rivulets running down her head and neck, she suddenly realized her headache had disappeared. The exercise must have helped ease her tension. "At least one good thing came out of this adventure," she muttered as she dried herself.

After a few weeks of dealing with her new hairstyle, which had grown enough that she could curl it more, Joelle had mastered the best techniques for blow-drying and styling her hair in a hurry. After it was curled, she slipped on the faithful black dress that managed to be both elegant and comfortable. Once her accessories were in place and she had spritzed perfume on her wrists, she was ready. Pleased with her reflection, she noticed she looked as good as she had when Wilbert first knocked on her front door hours ago.

As expected, Wilbert was already waiting for her when she had completed her toilette, just like Dean would have been. Wilbert's dark, brooding looks had their appeal, yet Joelle couldn't help but form an image of boyish-looking, auburn-haired Dean. She imagined his crooked smile. "Joelle, you take forever to get ready to go anywhere, but why? You always look gorgeous," Dean would say.

And she would reply, "Men are so lucky. You always look fantastic with no effort at all."

"Why, thank you."

Joelle jumped when Wilbert's deep voice responded. She hadn't realized she'd voiced her last thought aloud.

"You don't look so bad yourself." Wilbert flashed a smile.

"Oh!" Joelle felt the heat rise to her cheeks. "Thanks," she managed to say before navigating the conversation to calmer verbal waters. "We'd better get going if we want to see the play."

"You're right." He began walking.

"By the way, you never mentioned the name of the show. Although whatever it is, I'm sure I'll enjoy it," she hastened to add.

He chuckled. "I'm sure you will. It's *The Sound of Music.*"

"I've never seen that play performed live. I've only seen the Julie Andrews movie." On impulse, she belted out a few lines of the title tune. Swirling and skipping, she moved her hands as if controlling a full skirt.

"Brava, brava!" Laughing, Wilbert clapped as they reached the car. Wilbert once again remembered to open her door. "I don't promise the lead in this cast will be as talented as Julie Andrews. They're just local players. Most of them like to act and sing as a hobby, but the play should be good enough."

As Wilbert walked around his car, Joelle leaned over to unlock his door. She happened into an angle that gave her a good view of the backseat. There was a paper bag on the seat she hadn't noticed before. Two or three inches of a thin, pink tail poured out of the top. She hoped it wasn't what she thought it was.

"What's that?" she asked Wilbert as he slid into his seat.

"It's a possum," he said as he started the car.

Joelle cringed as she buckled her seat belt. Wilbert had confirmed her worst fears. "A possum? What are you doing with that nasty thing in the car?"

"I found him while I was mowing. He was already dead. Don't worry." Wilbert pointed his index finger forward as he steered. "There's a dumpster along the side of the road just a couple of miles up. I'm going to leave him there."

Joelle wrinkled her nose. She wished Wilbert had let his friend rest in peace.

True to his word, Wilbert stopped and threw the bag in the dumpster.

Joelle felt better. "I must say, this evening has involved the oddest detours I've ever been on."

"Didn't my personal ad promise excitement?"

"Hmm." Joelle thought back to the ad. "I do seem to remember something about variety, but nothing about excitement."

"If you have variety, doesn't excitement naturally come with the territory? Maybe I'm just getting the ad you read mixed up with the one I put in *Swinging Christian Singles,* then." Wilbert shot his eyes to her. "Just kidding, of course."

"As if I'd think there really was any such magazine." Joelle chuckled. At least Wilbert possessed a sense of humor. Maybe he could turn out to be someone she could like.

She peered out the windshield, enjoying the summer greenery and smooth passage over curved roads. They hadn't been driving long when Joelle felt a tickling sensation on her leg. She looked down and spotted a small brown insect hurrying toward the hem of her knit dress. Picking it off of her hose, she was appalled to see it was a small tick.

"Those weeds you had me chopping must be infested with more than rats." She held the bug between the nails of her forefinger and thumb.

"A sure sign of summer, though not my favorite," Wilbert agreed.

After rolling down the window, she evicted the offender. "No wonder you stuck me over in that corner." Her lips twisted before she spotted a bug on his sleeve. "Wait a minute. Looks like you managed to get a tick, too." She reached for the bug, retrieving it from his sleeve. Quickly, she tossed the second stowaway out of the window.

"Thanks. Looks like nobody's immune today."

No sooner had Joelle rolled up the window than she spotted two more ticks on her legs and another on her arm. Thankfully, none of them had laid claim to a place to bite, but Joelle was unsettled all the same. "I checked for ticks when I showered. I thought for sure I didn't have one on me anywhere."

Wilbert flicked one from his pants leg. "Same here. What could be going on?"

Joelle had a disturbing thought. "The possum. Wonder if that's where they're coming from?"

"But I didn't have him in the car anytime

at all, and he's long gone now."

"He must have been in here long enough to leave us with a few souvenirs."

Wilbert rolled down his window as he spotted yet another offending insect. "Maybe you're right. It's not easy for me to concentrate on driving with all these ticks everywhere."

"And on my best dress, too." She tried not to sound too disagreeable.

Even though he kept his hands on the steering wheel, Wilbert's shoulders sank. "I hate to say this, Joelle, but I wonder if —"

"We should call it a night?"

He nodded slowly, demonstrating his reluctance.

"Maybe we'd better. I hate to agree since you've spent money on the tickets."

"The money will be wasted in any event, if we can't enjoy the show."

Joelle sighed. "You're right."

Without saying another word, Wilbert took advantage of the next driveway and used it to make a three-point turn. They were soon headed back in the direction of Joelle's house.

"I feel terrible about this, Joelle. I really wanted us to have a good time," Wilbert apologized.

"Don't worry about it."

"If only I hadn't picked up that possum."

"There's no point in beating yourself up. You can't turn the clock back now."

"Oh, the comfort of clichés." He chuckled.

Joelle giggled. "I guess that's why they're clichés."

He shot her a glance and returned his gaze to the road. "I'll make this up to you, Joelle. We'll do something special one night. I don't know yet what that will be, but I'll think of something."

"Don't worry. You don't owe me anything."

The rest of the drive was silent as Joelle watched for ticks and tried to keep Wilbert from being bitten, too. Of all the dates she'd had, this evening had to be the biggest bust of all.

Folding her arms, Joelle stared at the road. Though a native of the mountains, she still tended to get carsick if she didn't look up when taking a long drive over the deep curves. Not many cars met them on the remote road, so when she spotted a silver sedan, Joelle took notice.

That can't possibly be Dean. What would he be doing out here, especially this late in the evening? She gave herself a mental tap on the head. *Stop being so silly. Dean doesn't own the only silver sedan in the world. Or even in Virginia.*

Still, she looked closely at the couple as they approached. The driver looked too much like Dean for her to dismiss her suspicions. Though both cars were moving fast, she tried to get a good look at the passenger. The woman certainly wasn't Dean's carrot-topped sister, Mandy. Dark hair, overdone in a sexy feather cut looked like — no, it couldn't be. She gasped.

Nicole?

As the car passed, Joelle turned her head and watched until its taillights were out of view.

"Someone you know?" Wilbert asked.

"I'm afraid so." Turning back in her seat, Joelle pouted. She had a bone to pick with Mr. Dean Nichols.

CHAPTER 8

As soon as she hopped out of Wilbert's car, Joelle walked over the flagstone path to the porch, dropped her bag loaded with her dirty T-shirt and jeans, and rushed into the house. She hadn't cleared the living room before she heard her dad calling from the den, over the blare of a television news broadcast. "Is that you, Joelle?"

"It's me," she called back.

"Home already?"

By this time, she was halfway down the back hall. "Yes, sir."

"Everything okay?" he shouted.

She stuck her head in the door of the den on her way to her bedroom. "Fine. I'll tell you about it later."

After rushing through her room and into the bathroom, she hurried to shed her dress. Soon she had showered for a second time within the span of an hour. Joelle figured she was the cleanest woman in town. She grabbed a clean maroon T-shirt and an old pair of loose gray athletic shorts from the dresser drawer and put them on. After retrieving the formal outfit she had shed from the bathroom floor, Joelle dashed out of the front door and gathered her bag. Several more steps around the side of the dwelling took her to the backyard.

Now that the infested clothes were safely out of the house, Joelle moved a bit more slowly. After reaching the outdoor shed, she snatched a can of tick spray from one of the shelves. Then she hung her canvas tennis shoes, jeans, T-shirt, good black dress, hose, and underthings on the clothesline. Using the can of spray, Joelle saturated each garment to be sure no bug would survive.

Her mother came up behind her. "What in the world are you doing?"

"I'm getting rid of ticks. I got them all in my clothes."

"Of course you can expect a few bugs to be out this time of year, but aren't you overdoing it a bit? And on your good dress, too. That reminds me." She checked her watch. "Why are you home already? You couldn't possibly have had time to clean a churchyard and see a play, to boot."

Joelle rolled her eyes. "Wilbert put a dead possum in the car. He dumped it out, but not before the ticks that were on it got all over the car and us."

"A possum? *Ewww!*"

"Needless to say, we had to call the evening off."

"Too bad. He seemed nice enough."

"Who seemed nice enough? Wilbert, or the possum?" Joelle joked.

With an appreciative chuckle, her mother put her hands on still slim hips and watched the clothes sway in the mild summer breeze. "So will you and Wilbert be seeing each other again?"

Making plans for another date, especially with Wilbert, was the last thing Joelle wanted to consider at the moment. "I have no idea, Mom." She turned her attention to her clothes. Detecting a dry spot on her jeans, she misted it with the poison.

"After all that spray, I'm sure no insect in this world would dare come within a foot of the clothesline."

"Let's hope not," said Joelle.

"You know, I hate to mention this," Eleanor said, arms folded over her chest, "but you probably didn't need to put all that insecticide all over everything. You could have just run the clothes through the washer and then let them spin in the dryer for about a half hour."

She turned to her mother. "Oh." Still holding the can of poison, Joelle felt a bit foolish. "Really?"

"Really." Eleanor smiled her knowledge-able, yet comforting, smile — the one that must be taught at the secret school for mothers where universal knowledge is imparted sometime during every woman's first pregnancy. "But at least by spraying you'll be sure to kill them all."

"That's right." Joelle was glad her mother allowed her to save face.

"You must have gotten into a mess of ticks to be so hyper."

"You wouldn't believe it." Sighing, she looked at the garments hanging on the line. "I guess now the only thing to do is let these clothes hang out until tomorrow morning."

"While you're waiting, you can read your mail." Eleanor handed Joelle two envelopes and several mail-order clothing catalogs. "I forgot to give it to you earlier."

Joelle took the parcels. "That's all right. I didn't have time to read it before now, anyway."

After depositing the can back on its shelf in the shed, Joelle walked back toward her house. The path to the cement patio mean-dered through the expansive backyard. Carpeted with green grass, the yard had hosted many good times. Joelle remembered games of hide-and-seek, catching lightning bugs at dusk after long summer days, years of birthday parties, even one brother's wedding. At the far end of the plot was her mother's garden. The patch of land she called her own offered time alone to commune with God and to feel pride in watching her vegetables grow. Thanks to their mother, summer at the Jamisons' meant garden-fresh corn on the cob, green beans, and tomatoes.

Lifting her eyes to her bedroom window, Joelle watched the floral chintz curtains sway back and forth with the breeze sweeping through the screen. She thought about her happy years in that room. Joelle had never lived anywhere else for more than a few months. Her parents had bought the three-bedroom white frame house two years after they were wed. All their adult lives had been spent there. She imagined that no matter how old she grew, the Jamison residence would always feel like home. One day, Joelle hoped the house she and her husband — whoever he turned out to be — would have would be able to give their children the same sense of belonging and security.

Flipping through the mail as she walked, she noticed the return address on one letter was from the bank. Probably her savings account statement. That could wait until she was at her desk with her records nearby. Riffling past it, she noticed the second envelope was from a man who certainly would never be her husband. Lloyd Newby. "I don't believe it."

"Don't believe what?" Joelle's mother asked as she seated herself on the floral-patterned glider.

Joelle sat on the freestanding wooden swing and began moving back and forth. "This letter. It's from Lloyd Newby. You remember him."

She nodded. "The one who stuck you with the restaurant tab?"

"The one and only." Ripping open the envelope, Joelle was surprised to find a card. On the front was a photograph of a pouting baby. Inside was the word "Sorry." Lloyd had simply signed his name on the bottom. Even more surprising was Lloyd's check taped to the inside. It was written for $250, more than enough to cover the cost of their evening together.

What wasn't a surprise from a man so bent on keeping up appearances was the expensive lettering and fancy additions Lloyd had ordered to embellish his checks. His name and address were printed in an elegant blue script. The letter N, also in an elaborate script, appeared beside his name and address. The check itself appeared pale blue at first blush, but upon closer inspection, Joelle saw it pictured a sea and sky. The words "Ride the Wave of Success!" were emblazoned near the name of his bank.

Joelle held up the check for her mother to inspect. "Well, what do you know? He kept his word after all."

Eleanor's blond eyebrows rose. "I'll say. He certainly spared no expense on the check itself."

"That's Lloyd. Always showing off."

"Even so, I'm as surprised as you are that he paid you back." She folded her arms. "Especially since he's apparently fond of wasting money."

A grin tickled Joelle's lips. Her mother thought paying good money for embellished checks was foolish when her bank offered plain ones free of charge.

"That goes to show, you can't always tell about people," said Eleanor.

"I'll be telling Dean all right. He was sure I'd never get my money back." Joelle relished the thought of talking to Dean. She had to let him know he had been wrong about Lloyd. The check proved he was wrong. She wasn't such a poor judge of character.

"That reminds me. You remember how the phone was ringing when you were leaving the house? Well, it turned out to be Dean."

Joelle's heart skipped a beat. She let her hands fall to her lap. "Dean? Why didn't you tell me? I would have come back into the house and taken his call."

"What do you mean, you would have come back in the house? You were already out on your date."

"Such as it was," Joelle muttered.

"You didn't know at the time it would turn out to be a disaster. But anyways," Eleanor waved her hand as if swatting an annoying fly, "why would you stop everything just to talk to him? You always have said he's just a friend. Can't he talk to you anytime?"

"I — I guess. Um, you don't know what he wanted, do you?"

"He said something about having tickets to a show. I don't know what show it was."

The cogs in Joelle's brain began turning. She wondered if Dean had indeed been on his way to see the same play she and Wilbert had abandoned. If so, that would explain why their cars passed on the road. An unwelcome thought occurred to her. "You didn't tell him I was out on a date

127

with someone else, did you?"

"I don't think so. I didn't see any need. I just said you were out for the evening, and I wasn't sure when you'd be home."

"What did he say then?"

"Nothing, really. Although, I could tell he was disappointed. He did say for you to call if you got back before eight." Eleanor gave her daughter a pat on the knee. "You know, you were better off not being home anyway. Even if Dean is just a friend, there's no need in you looking like you're not popular enough to be out on a Friday night."

It was Joelle's turn to roll her eyes. "Dean and I are close enough that we don't need to play games."

"Is that so?" Eleanor's lips pursed. "Can a man and a woman ever really be just friends?"

Joelle didn't want to answer. Her mother's oblique suggestion was too unsettling to contemplate, but so was the alternative. Now that she knew Dean had tickets to the play, she was certain of two facts. One, Dean was the one she and Wilbert had met on the road. Two, the woman with him had to be Nicole — not that it mattered. Whoever Dean saw was his business. But she wouldn't wish Nicole on her worst enemy, much less her best friend. If only she'd answered the phone before she left!

"And anyhow," her mother said, interrupting her thoughts, "if I had run out the door and hollered for you to come to the phone to speak to Dean, would that have changed anything?"

"Maybe."

"I don't see how. Unless you're trying to make me believe you would have left this Wilbert fellow standing out there on the front porch so you could go to the play with Dean instead."

"Well . . ."

"Well, nothing," Joelle's mother said with a wag of her finger. "Can't you see you're better off the way things turned out? If you'd answered the phone, you would have been forced to turn him down. You would have been cornered into telling him the whole truth. This way, he's just guessing."

"You have a point."

"Maybe you'll end up with Wilbert and Dean fighting over you." Eleanor chuckled.

"I doubt that." Joelle folded her arms. All that work, and she didn't even get to see the play. Not to mention her best black dress had become tick-infested. She wondered if she'd ever be able to get out the smell of insecticide. "After tonight, I have no intention of seeing Wilbert again. Ever."

She nodded once to emphasize her determination. "Things wouldn't have been so bad if we had actually gotten to the theater, but I did all that work for nothing."

"Work done for the church is never for nothing. Even if it's not for your own church, what you did tonight helped others in the Christian community," Joelle's mother pointed out.

A sense of shame washed over her. "You're right. I do need an attitude adjustment."

"You've had a hard night. Tomorrow things will look better. Maybe then you can think about giving Wilbert another chance."

"You like him that much?"

Eleanor shrugged. "I don't know him. He's obviously involved in his church, so if I were you, I'd be willing to go out with him a second time if he calls."

"I don't know. Mom, even without the ticks, the evening was a disaster. I can tell all he really wants is a maid."

"I know the evening wasn't much fun, but it wasn't Wilbert's fault." After Joelle shot her a look, Eleanor added, "All right. Maybe it was his fault, but at least the incident with the possum wasn't intentional. I feel sorry for him. He'll be trying to get ticks out of his car from now until the first winter freeze." Eleanor covered her mouth to stifle a laugh.

Her comment brought to Joelle's mind an image of Wilbert attempting to get rid of the pests. In spite of herself, Joelle joined her mother's laughter. Funny, she wished Dean were there to share it with them.

CHAPTER 9

The next evening was Singles' Night. As members of the group filed in one by one and began conversations, they happily chatted without regard to the time. Just before the meeting was ready to kick off, Zach entered. With him were two teenagers he introduced as his twin cousins. Radical styles of clothing and accessories caused the adolescent boys to be noticeable among their working-age elders.

The group tried to greet them with open arms, but the boys were reticent. Spurning attempts at conversation, they turned away and talked between themselves.

"Looks like our guests are here under duress," Joelle whispered to Zach.

"I know," Zach answered. "I hated to put you guys out by bringing them, but since they're in town, my mom insisted. She even bribed me with a steak dinner so I'd drive to her house to pick them up." Zach studied his young charges. A worried look entered his eyes then sat upon his face. He shook his head and returned his gaze to Joelle. "I think she just might have wanted to get rid of them for an evening."

Joelle wondered if Zach didn't speak the truth. Raven took his name to heart. His long, straight hair was dyed an ebony that contrasted with his pale skin like coal buttons against a snowman's body. The goatee he was attempting to grow was dark brown. Joelle assumed he sported the facial hair to look older, but in actuality, the goatee made him appear younger. Raven's T-shirt was solid black, as were his pants. Black boots covered his feet in defiance of the warm weather.

The fact that Eagle's long, platinum blond hair didn't occur naturally was betrayed by deep brown roots that matched his long sideburns. A black leather vest partially concealed a white T-shirt with writing that Joelle couldn't decipher. Black leather pants and boots covered the lower half of his body. No jewelry was spared. Several gold hoops decorated the lobes of each ear. On his right wrist was a gold ID bracelet. The other, in a bow to practicality, bore a watch.

Joelle hated to judge by appearances, but their style of dress made it difficult to draw any conclusion other than that they were trouble. She tilted her head and set her own eyes on the ceiling as though she were in deep contemplation. "Hmm. Wonder why your mom would want an evening without the twins?"

"I wonder." Zach shook his head.

As she and Zach were exchanging quips, Joelle kept an eye on Dean. The time was almost ten minutes after the hour. Dean consulted his watch every few seconds. In the meantime, Joelle took a head count. On the green couch sat the twins. Dean, Fiona, and Ashlynn occupied the multisectional pit group seating that rounded one corner. Zach sat beside her in one of two wing chairs with matching but worn brown vinyl upholstery. Who was missing?

Nicole! Joelle's heart gave her a sinking feeling.

At that moment, Dean spoke to the group. "Where's Nicole?"

"Nicole? I don't know for sure," Fiona answered, "but remember last week how she said something about having other plans?"

"She did? I don't remember that," said Dean.

"I do," Ashlynn countered. "She said she wouldn't be here this week."

"I wish I'd heard her," Dean remarked.

Dean wasn't even bothering to conceal his interest in Nicole! Joelle felt her heart's rapid beating betray her.

"I thought for sure she'd be here," Dean continued. "It was her turn to be in charge of the lesson and entertainment tonight."

Joelle didn't answer. The uncomfortable reality was, she didn't miss Nicole at all. If she were to admit the whole truth, Joelle was pleased that Nicole was absent.

"She's been really busy at work. I'm sure she forgot she promised to be in charge of the program." Zach's tone of voice indicated he didn't believe his own words.

Dean's mouth twisted into an unhappy curve. "I guess there's no other choice. I'll just have to wing it. We were supposed to talk about the Great Commission tonight. As for fun, you know me — I don't go anywhere without my guitar, so we can have some music later if anybody's interested."

A round of agreeable murmurs filled the room.

"You can practice your solo for tomorrow," Joelle observed. "We'll be your guinea pigs."

Dean winked. "Only if you promise to sing along."

Despite the teasing gesture, Joelle knew Dean wasn't joking. Joelle had developed her singing voice during high school with three years of lessons. At one time, she'd considered music as a career. After some contemplation, she decided she wasn't committed enough to the field to make it a profession. A steady job in accounting and bookkeeping seemed more appealing. Her associate degree in business management hadn't let her down. In the meantime, Joelle enjoyed singing as a hobby.

Joelle wondered why Nicole had skipped out on her commitment and left the group stranded. *At least now I look dependable, and she looks flighty.*

As soon as the thought entered Joelle's mind, a pang of guilt stabbed her. Allowing her own jealousy to get in the way was wrong. Nicole needed the church.

But I'm not jealous. I just know she's not right for Dean. That's all.

"You didn't know we had our own musical ensemble, did you, guys?" Zach told his cousins, Eagle and Raven.

"I can strum a few tunes," Dean said, "but I doubt I can compete with Hollywood."

"It's not like I'm up for a Dove Award or a Grammy, either," added Joelle.

"Don't worry about it. We're always on the listen out for new music," Eagle said. "We have our own band."

"Your own band? How exciting!" Ashlynn squealed, clasping her hands to her chest. "Have we heard of you?"

"We haven't gotten a deal with a major label yet," Eagle admitted.

"We haven't even gotten a deal with a minor label," Raven added. "We've sent our demo out to a lot of record companies, though. One day, somebody will notice us and give us a chance. Then, after we're stars, you'll be able to say you know the lead guitarist and vocalist — that's me — and the drummer — that's him over there," he said, pointing to his brother, "from PUG."

"Pug? Like the little dog?" Ashlynn wanted to know. "How cute!"

"Not really. It means Puked Up Garbage." Eagle's voice was filled with pride.

"Oh." A hint of a crestfallen expression crossed Ashlynn's face before she recovered and pasted on a smile. "I'd still be glad to listen to it sometime."

Still smiling, Ashlynn set her gaze on Zach. Though over the past few weeks he'd shown only vague signs of interest in the blue-eyed brunette, Ashlynn still tried to follow his interests and engage him in conversation whenever she could. Joelle was sure she knew the only reason Ashlynn offered to listen to the twins' music. Ashlynn hoped to parlay the experience into a chance to be near Zach.

"Don't pay any attention to them, Ashlynn," Zach said. "They like to get attention. A lot of what they say is for sheer shock value."

"Is not," Eagle protested.

"Don't think you're kidding anybody," Zach argued. "I know you love to say something shocking, just to see what people will do."

Dean tried to make peace. "It's a free country. You have the right to name your band whatever you want. Since you can read music, maybe you'd still like to play along with me. Did you bring your guitar, Raven?"

"I brought it out here, but I don't have it with me tonight."

"But you brought your vocal chords." Fiona smiled.

Eagle didn't respond to her lightheartedness with a smile of his own. "I don't know any hymns, and I don't want to learn any, either."

"We wouldn't be able to read the music, anyway. We don't write down our notes. We just remember them," Raven said. "Our music is alternative. We cover some songs by other groups, but mainly we write our own stuff. We don't play any religious songs."

"Sure we do." A reptilian smile covered Eagle's face.

"Not songs they'd like," Raven said. "You know that."

"What do you like to write about?" Dean inquired, keeping his facial expression and tone of voice friendly.

Raven shrugged. "Death. Suicide. How the world's an evil place, especially for teens like us."

"And how there is no God," Eagle added. Folding his arms, he offered them a daring look. The motion caused his shirt sleeve to move slightly. For the first time, Joelle noticed a tattoo on his forearm. The part she could see appeared to be the flat head and forked tongue of a cobra.

Joelle was all too aware of the popularity of tattoos. The body art came as no real surprise. Nevertheless, a warning from Leviticus 19 popped into Joelle's mind: *Ye shall not make any cuttings in your flesh for the dead, nor print any marks upon you: I am the LORD."*

Zach's voice interrupted into her musings. "That's enough, guys." He looked around the room, briefly making eye contact with each single. "I'm sorry if my cousins offend

139

you. As I said before, these guys like to play the role of agitators. It's part of their image. They don't mean most of what they say."

"Yes, we do," Eagle insisted. "The people who don't get it just aren't listening. Not to our music, and not to what we have to say."

"You'd be surprised by how people might listen if you'd drop the attitude." Though his words presented a challenge, the expression in Zach's eyes warned his cousins not to speak further.

Dean shot Joelle a look of unease. She knew he was wondering how Raven and Eagle would tolerate spending the evening amidst their group. She was about to find out.

CHAPTER 10

Putting on an optimistic expression, Dean turned to the teens. "I hope tonight's lesson will help change your minds."

"Don't count on it," Eagle said. "Everybody knows man invented God to explain where we came from, but modern science answered all those questions years ago. We don't need God anymore. Evolution explains it all."

"Is that what you think?" Dean asked without a trace of hostility. "Do you realize the theory of evolution is just that — a theory? It is not a proven fact."

"That's not what they say in biology class," Raven pointed out.

"Your teachers are trying their best to instruct you in what they believe to be the truth," Zach explained. "Unfortunately, some of them have been seriously misled."

"He's right," Dean agreed. "We were taught the same thing when we went to high school. Our teachers also looked exclusively to science for the answers, but all anyone needs is this." Holding up his book, Dean tapped his forefinger just under the words *Holy Bible,* imprinted in gold.

"That book does not have all the answers," Eagle argued. "If it did, we'd know why God lets evil happen."

"Just because God allows evil to happen doesn't mean He likes or approves of it," Joelle answered.

"True," Dean agreed. "Evil happens because we live in a fallen world. This is not the Garden of Eden."

"For once, something you say makes sense," said Raven.

"Eve made the mistake of listening to Satan and giving in to temptation. Today, all of us are just as human. We aren't perfect, either," Fiona elaborated.

Dean gazed unflinchingly into the teens' faces. "Some of us make a grave error. The error of not believing in Him."

"We have the privilege of not listening to Him." Eagle returned Dean's stare with a scowl.

"You're right," Dean conceded. "God gives us the free will to accept or reject Him."

"Really? Can you prove that?" Raven's

eyes held a light of interest for the first time that evening.

"That fact is both written and implied all through the Bible. Let me see." Dean opened his Bible and turned toward the back. "I think I can find one especially good passage in the book of Revelation."

"The book of Revelation?" Raven's expression became intense, as though he was trying to recall something. Suddenly, his mouth opened into a slight smile of triumph. He snapped his fingers and then lifted his index finger. "Is that the part where some dude has a bunch of weird dreams?"

"Some might say that." Chuckles filled the room, along with the sound of pages turning in four other Bibles.

Raven's blue eyes lit up for the first time. "Wicked awesome!"

In contrast, Eagle's gray eyes narrowed. His arms remained folded. "Mom says that's the fire and brimstone book."

"Fire and brimstone. Cool, dude." Relaxing, Raven leaned back into the sofa cushion.

"Sounds more like it's hot to me," Ashlynn joked. A round of good-natured groans and a few giggles followed.

Joelle glanced at Dean. Apparently oblivious to the conversation around him, he kept his eyes on the page, scrolling down the words as he read. A few moments passed before he tapped his finger on the passage.

"Here it is," he said. "I'll start reading at Revelation 21:6. This is Jesus speaking to John at Patmos. 'And he said unto me, It is done. I am Alpha and Omega, the beginning and the end. I will give unto him that is athirst of the fountain of the water of life freely. He that overcometh shall inherit all things; and I will be his God, and he shall be my son. But the fearful, and unbelieving, and the abominable, and murderers, and whoremongers, and sorcerers, and idolaters, and all liars, shall have their part in the lake which burneth with fire and brimstone: which is the second death.' "

Raven nudged his twin. "Mom was right. There is fire and brimstone in that book!"

"See, I told you God tries to force you to believe in Him. It's saying we'll be burned to death if we don't," Eagle said. "Or at least I think that's what it's saying. It's hard to understand. Nobody talks like that anymore. No wonder nobody I know reads the Bible."

"Believe it or not, other people feel the same way," Dean said. "There are other versions of the Bible that are easier to understand."

"I have the New International Version," Fiona offered.

"That might help. Would you read it?" Dean asked.

Fiona nodded. " 'He said to me: It is done. I am the Alpha and the Omega, the Beginning and the End. To him who is thirsty I will give to drink without cost from the spring of the water of life.' "

"That's a lie, man," Eagle interrupted. "There is a cost. They want you to go to church every Sunday and not have fun anymore."

"Church doesn't have to be boring. Services can be great, when you really want to worship the Lord," Zach pointed out. "And church isn't just for Sunday, either." He swept his hand over the room. "Being here tonight ought to show you that much. Look at how all of us here are friends."

Eagle surveyed the room. "I have more friends than this."

"Would they still be your friends if you started going to church?" Joelle wondered aloud.

The teenager's mouth opened with apparent surprise. He didn't respond right away. "I dunno," he said and dropped his gaze to the floor. His unwillingness to meet her eyes was answer enough for Joelle.

"Not so long ago, most of my friends were outside of the church, too," she explained. "But soon after I accepted Jesus as my personal Savior, a lot of them abandoned me."

Eagle looked up. "If that's true, then your friends weren't as loyal as mine."

His words cut too close. Without warning, an unwelcome tide of ill feeling engulfed Joelle. She remembered each of her old friends. In her mind, she revisited the pain of their departures from her life as if each event had happened yesterday. The realization that they could no longer accept her now that she had begun a true relationship with the Lord still caused her to flinch with grief.

She swallowed. "I don't know your friends. So maybe you're right," Joelle conceded. "But I do know why a few of the people I called my friends broke off with me."

"Let me guess," Eagle scoffed. "You're going to tell me whether I want to know or not."

Joelle ignored his loaded comment. "A year ago, instead of being here tonight, I probably would have been at a club."

"I sure wish that's where I was right about now." Eagle voiced his protest with enough volume for Joelle to hear him, but softly enough to stay out of trouble with Zach.

Hiding her frustration, Joelle sent up a silent prayer to be infused with the Holy Spirit. After taking in a strengthening breath, she continued. "But now I don't go to those places anymore."

"Just like that, huh?" Raven's eyes grew wide. "Don't you miss the clubs?"

She flinched. "Sometimes, as much as I hate to admit it. You have to realize, I always called myself a Christian, but it was only within the past few months that I really let Christ change my life. I don't pretend I didn't have any trouble shedding my old life. I still have to die to it every day."

"Die to it?" asked Raven.

"Yes. I mean, I have to remember I promised to serve Jesus. I can't let my desire to go back to my old habits get in the way of my walk with the Lord."

"How do you do that?" he asked.

"I pray for strength each morning."

"When do you have the most trouble?" asked Ashlynn.

Joelle was surprised by the source of the inquiry, but she answered. "When I start thinking about my old friends and my old habits, it's usually because I'm lonely or just feeling down for some reason. Memories come back if I have reason to drive by one of my old haunts."

"What keeps you from stopping the car and going in?" she asked.

"Concentrating on the Lord. Praying to Him." Joelle paused. "I think about how little I've lost and how much I've gained. I've traded a few small, fleeting pleasures for solid, meaningful relationships in the Christian community and the ultimate reward — eternal life."

"What does that have to do with your friends?" Eagle prompted.

"I did wander off the subject, didn't I? Sorry," she apologized. "I found out that the friends who really were interested in me as a person are still in touch. The ones who just looked at me as a buddy to fill out a table at a club and to gossip with are the ones who dumped me, so they weren't friends at all. Not really."

Her own words caused Joelle to remember one friend in particular. Actually, he had been much more than a friend. Dustin was the man Joelle thought she'd marry one day. She had been both surprised and heartbroken when he was the first to drop her after she responded to the life-changing gospel.

Ever since she'd known him in high school, Dustin had professed to be a Christian. Joelle knew neither she nor Dustin had been living a godly life, but she always assumed they'd get their frivolous ways out of their systems, settle down, and then begin walking the talk. When Joelle accepted Christ, however, Dustin wasn't ready for the change. He was happy going on as before, giving religion lip service and attending church once or twice a year. A larger commitment proved too much. When Dustin promptly dumped her for someone else, Joelle unhappily discovered that he'd never intended to live anything remotely resembling a righteous life. At least her acceptance of the Lord showed her Dustin wasn't right for her.

A ray of hope surged through her. *Surely God will help me find a man through the Christian personals. I've got to keep trying!*

Rising from her seat, she spoke again. "Sure, I was sad to lose my old friends; but as I said, I made new friends. And my best friend since childhood stayed with me." Joelle stopped behind Dean. Smiling, she patted him on the shoulder. She let her hand rest there for a moment, feeling his warmth.

He brought his hand to hers, touching it for an instant. "I'd say we're closer than ever. Joelle knows I'll always be here for her, no matter what."

"So it was worth it," Raven said, his voice barely above a whisper. He looked above Joelle's head, as though he were looking toward heaven and seeing God for the first time.

In a flash, she realized the embarrassment of confessing her struggles and imperfections in front of her friends and two strangers had happened for a reason. Her confession may have reached the adolescent. "Yes," she affirmed, her voice strong. "Accepting Christ was worth everything."

All eyes shifted to Eagle. Unrepentant, he glowered at them all.

Fiona finally broke the silence. "Shall I keep reading, Dean?"

He nodded. "Please do."

" 'He who overcomes will inherit all this, and I will be his God and he will be my son. But the cowardly, the unbelieving, the vile, the murderers, the sexually immoral, those who practice magic arts, the idolaters and all liars — their place will be in the fiery lake of burning sulfur. This is the second death.' "

"The second death? Ooooh, I'm so scared." Lifting his hands, Eagle shook them in feigned fright.

"You'd better be, dude!" Raven's laughter belied his words.

Dean sighed. Joelle watched his shoulders slump ever so slightly with discouragement. She wished she could think of something helpful to say, but no words fell on her lips. Raven, and especially Eagle, wouldn't be easy for anyone to reach. Their looks alone showed that much — but at least Dean had tried.

"If it's all right with everyone, what if we let Nicole pick up next week's lesson on the Great Commission?"

"Commission?" Raven asked. "Isn't that when you sell something and somebody pays you part of the profit?"

"In the business world, yes," Zach answered. "But when we speak of the Great Commission in the context of the New Testament, we mean Jesus' command that we should share the good news of His saving grace with everyone."

"Bo–ring," Eagle interjected. He let out an exaggerated yawn.

"Eagle, that's enough." Signaling his growing impatience, Zach's voice was firmer than it had been all night. "I don't expect you to like what you're hearing, but you're a guest here. There's no reason to be rude."

"That's all right, Zach," Dean said amidst nods of agreement. "We've hit on so many topics, all of us probably have enough to chew on for this week." He glanced at his watch. "It's time to move along to the entertainment anyway." After setting his Bible on the small table right beside the couch, he got up and retrieved the guitar from the corner where he'd left it. Propping it on his knee, he asked, "What song would everyone like to sing?"

Eagle suggested several offensive titles that Joelle assumed were hard rock or alternative tunes. She could feel Dean's embarrassment and distress.

Ashlynn and Fiona named a couple of bland secular songs, only to meet with blank looks from the twins. As titles were shouted out, only to be discarded, the tension became palpable. Everyone discerned that no song the regular group suggested would please, or even placate, the rebellious boys.

"How about something simple? Maybe 'Jesus Loves Me,' " suggested Dean. "Everyone knows that song, right?" He eyed the teens.

"That's it. I'm not singing a song for little kids. I'm outta here!" Eagle rose from his seat. He headed to the door. When he reached it, he pounded it open with the palm of his hand. He stomped down the hall, heavy boots causing his footfalls to echo on the tile floor in the hallway. They heard the door slam behind him as he escaped to the outdoors.

Zach made no move to follow his cousin. "Sorry, you guys." Letting out an audible sigh, he set his elbows on his knees and leaned his head in his hands.

"That's all right. You're doing the best you can," Ashlynn consoled him.

"Do you think you'd better go after him?" Joelle asked.

Zach lifted his head. "No need. He's just gone out to smoke a cigarette."

"Or maybe something else." Raven's voice was barely audible.

A fresh wave of unease washed over the group.

"Raven," Zach asked, "why don't you go and see what he's up to?"

Clearly relieved by the suggestion, Raven nodded and headed outside.

As soon as they heard the front door shut, Zach spoke. "I'm sorry I've ruined this meeting by bringing them. I thought they'd be on their best behavior. I should have known better."

"You haven't ruined anything," Dean assured. "Meeting them has given us a chance to practice what we preach."

"We've started out with pretty hard cases," Zach said. "They haven't had it easy. Their parents divorced a couple of years ago. They aren't saved, so how can anyone expect their boys to be any better?"

A collective intake of breath was followed by utterings of compassion and understanding from the group.

"I feel led to pray." Dean extended both hands to grasp Joelle's on one side and Fiona's on the other. He didn't have to ask twice. Everyone clasped hands and joined in a circle. "Since the guys might come back any moment, I suggest we keep our petitions silent."

The young adults bowed their heads, each immersed in private communication with the Lord. All too soon, they heard the front door creak open, followed by the sound of someone approaching the classroom, until Raven finally burst upon the circle. His eyes were wide and wild.

"I can't find Eagle. He's gone!"

CHAPTER 11

"What do you mean, he's gone?" Zach asked. "He just left a few minutes ago. He's got to be out there somewhere."

"I don't know where. I looked all over the place. In the front, in the back, in the parking lot. Everywhere." Raven's voice had become high-pitched with obvious fright.

"Don't worry," said Dean. "Zach's right. He couldn't have gone far. Unless —" He turned to Zach. "He couldn't have taken a car, could he?"

"I didn't hear a motor start," Joelle said.

"Thank goodness. Joelle, I'd like for you, Fiona, and Ashlynn to stay here," Dean instructed, pointing to each woman as he said her name, "just in case he decides to come back. If he does, one of you can stay with Eagle while the other two find us."

Joelle nodded. Secretly she hoped she wouldn't be the one who had to stay with Eagle. The prospect of handling a rebellious teen wasn't something she relished.

Unaware of Joelle's concerns, Dean turned to the other males. "Raven, you look through the forest in back of the church. Zach, why don't you and I take our cars and head off in both directions?"

Nodding, everyone began to put Dean's plan into place.

Joelle touched Dean on the shoulder. "Be careful," she whispered.

"I will." He gave her a sad smile. Joelle knew he blamed himself for Eagle's flight.

As soon as they left the church, Ashlynn said, "This night sure has been a disaster."

"It's not a disaster yet, and it only will be if they don't find Eagle," Joelle said.

Fiona smirked. "You say that as though finding Eagle would be a good thing."

"Fiona, you're so bad!" Ashlynn mocked.

She shrugged. "They might find him in jail. I'm sure he's got drugs on him."

Joelle sighed. "I feel sorry for him. For both of them."

"I don't," said Fiona, plopping herself into a comfortable chair. "They're troublemakers."

Though Ashlynn remained standing, Joelle sat on the adjacent couch. "But look where they come from. It can't be easy to conform when you don't have any support from your parents."

"Oh, stop blaming the parents, Joelle," Fiona sneered. "My parents divorced when I was in junior high. I didn't use that as an excuse to be a juvenile delinquent or to run away from God."

"But didn't your parents at least take you to church when you were little? Didn't you have a chance to learn about Jesus?"

Fiona's lips narrowed into a thin line. "Yes, they did. I have to admit that."

"From all appearances, these kids didn't have that chance. Can't you see they have no relationship with God at all? How can you run away from Someone you never knew?"

"I guess you're right."

"Good," Ashlynn interrupted. "Now instead of wasting time arguing, why don't we pray?"

"That's the second good suggestion we've had all night," Joelle said.

The three women joined together in good-natured chuckles before turning serious. Joining hands, they stood in a tight triangle and prayed aloud for the safe return of all involved.

Dean hopped into his car and started the engine. He paused for a moment before pulling out of the gravel parking lot. "Dear Lord," he prayed, "please guide me as I search for Eagle. Keep him in Your care, that he doesn't run into any wild animals or anyone who will hurt him. Help me to find him, then be with me as I bring him back to Zach. In the holy name of Your Son, amen."

After exiting the lot, Dean felt led to make a left turn. The country road was so narrow, two cars passing could easily sideswipe each other. Hairpin curves didn't help matters. Even though Dean had driven over this road time and time again, he had no choice but to keep his speed down. "Eagle was on foot," Dean reasoned to himself. "He couldn't have gone far." He had a disturbing thought. "Unless someone picked him up."

The road was never heavily traveled, but since Saturdays were busy with people running errands, going out on dates, and getting together with family and friends, the probability that Eagle had encountered someone was high. He groaned. "He might have made it to town by now." If he had money with him, Eagle could have hitched a ride into town, found the bus station, and bought a ticket for who knew where.

Dean consulted the digital clock on the

dash, noting that a half hour had passed since Raven told them his brother was missing. That meant Eagle had about a forty-five-minute head start. "If one of us doesn't find him soon, we could lose him altogether."

Nervousness caused his stomach to lurch. Zach was Dean's friend, and Dean would never do anything to hurt Zach. He felt responsible for Eagle's outburst. If any harm fell upon Eagle, how would he face Zach? How could they both tell Zach's mother the awful news? No. Eagle had to stay safe. Dean had to find him. "Please, Lord, keep Eagle from going too far!"

Dean scanned the countryside. Night had fallen in full force, covering the earth with a blanket as black as Eagle's leather vest. Remembering Eagle's ebony boots, Dean held no hope that he'd be able to spot a thin glow-in-the-dark strip of light on athletic shoes meant to protect nighttime joggers. He'd just have to be vigilant in looking for movement and for any form that could be a human.

Realizing that Eagle might not be walking along the road, he peered into the surrounding forest. The trees had long since budded. Their branches were now laden with leaves that were impossible to see through. But he had to keep searching for Eagle.

Though he tried to investigate each side of the road while driving, Dean had a feeling Eagle wouldn't venture into the forest. Since he was used to concrete and city lights, the boy most likely would feel more comfortable staying with the road. Eagle put on a brave front, but Dean wasn't confident the scrawny teenager would want to go head-to-head with the occasional black bear that roamed these parts.

After driving several more minutes at a pace not unlike a tortoise, Dean gave up. "I'll just have to turn around in the Nelsons' driveway," he muttered, thinking aloud. "I guess then I'll go back by the church and try the other direction."

Rounding the next curve, Dean concentrated his gaze on the right side of the road. The Nelsons' driveway was marked by a black mailbox that tended to vanish into the night. If he wasn't careful, he'd miss it and would be forced to drive another mile or so before he could make a three-point turn in safety.

The headlights had just beamed on the mailbox when Dean detected movement a few feet beyond. His heart beat in rapid rhythm. "That looks like Eagle!"

Slowing down even more, Dean's headlamps illuminated the figure. Blond hair straggled midway over a black vest. White T-shirt sleeves extended over tattooed arms. In one hand was a lighted cigarette. "That's got to be him."

The object of Dean's attention stopped walking and spun on his heel. To Dean's relief, he stared into the expressionless face of Eagle. The boy placed the cigarette between unsmiling lips. His left hand tucked into his pants pocket, with his free hand he stuck out his thumb, waving it proudly in the night.

"Yeah!" Now Dean had every reason to stop. Passing Eagle by only a few feet, he eased his vehicle to the edge of the road, letting the tires on the passenger side glide onto the shoulder. Unable to pull his car completely off the road, Dean put the car in park and hoped no one else would choose that moment to speed by.

After reaching the car in haste, Eagle opened the passenger door, dropped his cigarette, and smashed it with his foot. "I need a ride to —" A look of recognition and horror crossed his face. "It's you!"

Seeing Eagle's fright, Dean leaned over and tried to grab him. Eagle proved too fast. Leaving the door open, the boy fled in the opposite direction.

Dean wasn't about to give up. He killed the engine, opened his door, and hopped out, quickly shutting it behind him. Eagle's dark clothes didn't keep Dean from spying the youth as he fled toward the Nelsons' driveway.

Dean soon overtook him. Eagle was at least thirteen years younger, but he wasn't fit enough to shake off Dean, who kept in shape by running three miles a day. At that moment, he was grateful that he had put in the time running each morning. As soon as he got within arm's reach of Eagle, he grabbed him by the vest.

Eagle tried to escape but didn't think quickly enough to shrug out of his vest. In a flash, Dean reached out and grabbed his arm. Eagle writhed and attempted to hit Dean with his other fist. Dean adroitly stepped out of the way of the swinging hand. Twisting Eagle's arm behind his back finally subdued the teenager. He became still.

"Okay. I give." Eagle's breathing was hard. "Will you let go of me?"

"I won't let go, but I will stop twisting your arm," Dean promised.

"Okay." His ragged breathing became slower.

Dean untwisted Eagle's arm, keeping both

hands in a vise-like grip around his undeveloped biceps. For an instant, Eagle started writhing again, but Dean tightened his hold. Apparently seeing the futility of fighting further, Eagle stopped.

"Had enough?" Dean asked.

Eagle nodded, glowering all the while.

"As long as you don't fight me, we'll get along just fine."

Eagle scowled but acquiesced and kept pace with Dean as he led him back to the car. Suddenly, the youth looked at him with a surprised expression. "Hey, you're not even breathing hard. What's up with you? Are you a pro basketball player or something?"

"Hardly." Dean chuckled in spite of himself. At five feet, eight inches in height, he wouldn't have made third string on his high school team, much less have a shot for a place on a professional team.

"I thought I could outrun somebody as old as you, no problem."

"Well, for one thing," Dean answered, "I don't smoke."

"All right. I'll get more than enough lectures when I get home. I don't need another one now."

Dean had no doubt Eagle was right. Unwilling to antagonize him further, Dean remained quiet as they drove back to the church. To his relief, Eagle didn't pull any more stunts in an effort to escape.

Grateful the teenager had been found, Dean said a silent prayer of thanks to the Lord.

The women were still praying when Dean arrived at church later, holding Eagle by the wrist.

"They're praying for me, aren't they?" The teen was seething with anger. "Tell them I don't want their prayers."

"Where did you find him?" Joelle asked.

"He'd made pretty good progress on foot. He was near the Nelson place, trying to hitch a ride." Dean looked at his young charge. "You weren't too happy when you found out the guy in the car was me, were you?"

"I knew you were old, but I didn't think you'd have a car that bogus," Eagle countered.

Joelle grinned in spite of herself. "You must not have thought it was too bogus, or else you wouldn't have tried to thumb a ride in it, would you?"

"I would have taken anything with a running engine at that point. I might have known I'd end up with just another do-gooder in this hick place."

"Now what?" Fiona asked.

"Don't worry about it," Eagle answered. "As soon as I get out of here, I'm calling Dad and telling him we're flying back to L.A. on the next plane out."

"I wasn't talking to you," Fiona said. "Dean, we can't leave the others out there all night, searching for him."

Dean looked at Eagle, then sent the women a glance that said Eagle was tough enough for him to handle, let alone them. "Joelle, why don't you call Zach from my cell phone? As for Raven, let's just wait. He promised not to stay in the forest longer than a half hour." He looked at his watch. "And that's almost passed now."

Time seemed to move slowly as the group, including one sullen teenager, waited. Eventually Raven returned, followed several minutes later by Zach.

As soon as Zach expressed relief that his young charge had been found, he switched gears. "Eagle, what did you think you'd accomplish by pulling a stunt like that?"

For once, Eagle had no comeback.

Zach took Eagle by the bicep and began leading him to the door. The spindly teen didn't try to resist his buff cousin. "Let's go."

CHAPTER 12

An hour later, Joelle and Dean were seated at a table in Mary's eatery. All around them were other diners. Most, like Joelle and Dean, were indulging in late evening desserts.

They both ordered comfort food — generous slices of lemon meringue pie and two mugs of decaffeinated coffee. Dean made small talk until their desserts were set before them. Dean hadn't made a display of his feelings as long as he'd remained at the church. Once they were alone, however, he was honest with Joelle about what he was really thinking.

"I wish I'd done a better job of reaching those kids." Dean didn't look at her, but stirred his coffee more than necessary to dissolve two spoonfuls of sugar. "If only I could have said something to break through. I had the best of intentions, and even then I ended up losing Eagle." His mouth curved into a frown. "Literally."

Joelle reached across the table and patted the hand Dean had wrapped around his mug. "You can't go blaming yourself, Dean. I thought you were great, all things considered."

"Thanks." He began cutting into his pie. Joelle could see that the cheap fork easily slid through the crust, which flaked all over the unadorned, but serviceable, cream-colored dessert plate.

"Pulling off a lesson and entertainment without notice is no easy feat," Joelle added.

"I could have done a much better job if I'd been prepared." Dean lifted his overloaded fork halfway to his lips. "I wish Nicole had been more considerate. I can't believe how she left all of us hanging high and dry like that. Eagle and Raven must think we're the most disorganized group they've ever seen." He placed the pie in his mouth and chewed, although he looked too upset to enjoy the treat.

"I don't know about that. I doubt very seriously Nicole would have had a better lesson, even with prepared materials. She just doesn't have your experience, and she sure isn't anywhere near where you are in her faith walk." Copying her dining companion, Joelle indulged in a bite of her own pie.

"Thanks for the compliment, but comparing my behavior to others' isn't the way to go about deciding how to conduct myself." He sighed. "Not to mention it's obvious that Raven and Eagle think I'm a boring old adult with my mellow acoustic guitar. Wonder if they realized before tonight that not all guitars come with amplifiers."

"I doubt it." Joelle laughed. "They think we're all a bunch of Jesus freaks. And you know what? They would have thought that no matter what. You have nothing to be embarrassed about. Nothing that went wrong tonight was your fault."

Dean shook his head. "I let Zach down."

"No, you didn't. If Zach were here, he'd be the first to agree with me." Joelle set her fork on the edge of her plate. "If anything, he'd say he let you down by bringing the boys, and then by not keeping them in line once they got there."

Dean moved his mug in a series of circles, swirling the hot coffee. "Maybe Eagle would have stayed if I'd delivered a more effective lesson and played some songs he knew."

Joelle swallowed a tiny portion of pie. "What are you trying to say? That if you had known they were coming, you would

168

have bought an electric guitar and learned a bunch of hard rock songs just to please them? Or maybe have even gotten a tattoo?" She shook one finger at him, letting it wave once with each word. "I don't think so."

"I assure you, the tattoo would have been one of those temporary ones that comes off the next day. Nothing too radical, either. Maybe just a heart." He flashed the endearing smile she had loved for so many years.

"What? You wouldn't have picked one that said 'Mother'? Your poor mom would be disappointed." She clicked her tongue in mock derision. He laughed along with her. "I'm just glad Ashlynn didn't find out Zach was bringing his cousins," Joelle observed. "If she'd known in advance they look like hard-core rockers, she probably would have worn leather clothes and covered her hair with a spiked wig. She might have even used henna tattoos on her arms and ankles." Joelle shook her head. "Anything to impress Zach."

"As if she would actually trade in her smooth Twila Paris and Rachael Lampa CDs for bone-jarring alternative music."

Joelle chuckled. "Maybe the boys would have been more comfortable the night we played Twister."

"I doubt it. My guess is they would have

thought that game was silly, too."

"Probably," she admitted. "But there's no point in saying 'woulda, shoulda, coulda' now. We can't go back and change the meeting, and we shouldn't have to. We can't be expected to tailor our evenings to please everyone."

Dean thought for a moment. "You know something? You're right. I wouldn't have changed a thing. Even if I had tried, they would have been able to tell I was putting on an act. Secular folks can spot hypocrisy in Christians faster than we can see it in each other. Or ourselves." He drank a swallow of coffee and set the mug back down on the table. "But I feel bad that those boys didn't feel comfortable with us. I mean, when someone literally runs away and tries to hitch a ride somewhere else, that's saying a lot about your hospitality . . . and it's all negative."

"Eagle's problems didn't begin tonight, Dean. His running away like that is the result of many years of alienation."

A trace of a grin touched his lips. "Sounds like an accurate diagnosis, Ms. Psychologist. Too bad he couldn't have waited one more night before deciding to act upon his feelings."

"You would have blamed yourself, any-

170

way." Joelle finished her coffee.

"True."

"I don't think we can count their boredom as our failure. You can't expect everyone who walks into our church — or any church — to become converted instantly. Raven and Eagle are very, very far from the Lord. They're living a totally different lifestyle. Although," she said thoughtfully, "I think I saw a glimmer of interest in Raven."

He nodded, his eyes alight with hope for the first time that evening. "I thought so, too. Let's just pray it's not short-lived."

"Just like the parable of the seeds?" she ventured. "You're afraid your words may have fallen on rock?"

"Precisely. Even if Raven's interest is piqued, he still hasn't made a commitment to Christ. At least, he didn't say so."

"It's too soon," she pointed out.

"You're right." He twisted his paper napkin around his fingers, although his faraway expression indicated he was too absorbed in contemplation to be conscious of his gestures. After a moment, he returned his full attention to Joelle. "Even if he tries to change, he has no motivation to alter his behavior once he gets back to L.A. He'll still be playing in the band with Eagle, and he won't have Zach bringing him to church."

"Are you sure Zach will bring him to church again after tonight?"

"He won't have a chance. The boys fly back to L.A. this week."

"Too bad. It would have been good to have another chance to reach them, although I don't know how far anyone can get with Eagle at this point. He seems set against the Lord." Joelle sighed. "I'm sure God has plans for Eagle and Raven. When the time is right, He will reveal them. In the meantime, we should just be glad we were able to plant some seeds."

Joelle watched as Dean took a few more bites of pie. He didn't speak for awhile but seemed to be concentrating on private thoughts rather than the taste of the dessert. She wondered if he'd even remember consuming the pie once he left the diner. Joelle didn't mind the silence. After years together, she and Dean were comfortable just being in each other's presence.

She had just finished her own dessert when Dean finally spoke. "How are things at home?"

"Wonderful. Mom finally took her GED test."

"That's great," Dean agreed. "She's been wanting to get her diploma for a long time now. I'm sure she's glad to get the test over with."

"You said it."

"How does she think she did?"

"She says she doesn't know, but of course she did fine." She leaned toward him. "After she gets her diploma, we're planning a surprise party for her. You'll be invited, but don't say anything about it."

"I wouldn't think of missing it." Dean glanced at his watch. "It's getting late. I'd better be hitting the road. I need to get some rest if I plan to sing that solo tomorrow in church." He snapped his fingers. "Oh, I almost forgot. The choir director wanted me to ask you if you'd sing a solo sometime."

Joelle moved her plate aside and propped her elbows on the table. She leaned closer to Dean. "She couldn't ask me herself?"

"Maybe she thinks I have some influence." He arched his eyebrows playfully.

She let her mouth curl into a coy grin. "Maybe you do."

"Does that mean you're willing to sing? I don't think she cares what the song is, as long as either Marla can play it on the organ or you can get a tape."

Joelle thought about the prospect of singing in front of the church. Mixed emotions of happiness, anticipation, and uncertainty reared their heads. She let out a sigh. "I don't know, Dean. I feel so unworthy, with my conversion so recent."

"No one else in the congregation thinks that way," he assured her. "If anything, now is the best time for you to sing His praises. Your outlook is fresh and new, unlike some of us who've been heavily involved in the work of the church all of our lives."

She was still unsure. Getting up in front of the whole church to sing by herself seemed daunting. An idea popped into her head. "You know, I like that Crystal Lewis song 'Beauty for Ashes.' "

"I know that song." He nodded. "That tune should work well with your voice."

"And your voice, too. Why don't you sing it with me?"

"A duet?"

"I think that's what they call it," she teased.

"I don't know. . . ."

She put on her best woeful face. "Please? I'd like having you there to help me sing. I know I'll have a lot more confidence that way."

"We do make beautiful music together," he noted.

Joelle wondered if he realized that statement could work on two levels. She decided she'd better head for safer verbal waters. "I like the words. All about how God gives us something for nothing."

" 'For our ashes, He gives us beauty. Strength for fear.' "

"See? You already know the lyrics."

He stopped as if considering her offer. "All right. I'll do it."

"Great!" Joelle felt better already.

"When is the best time for you to practice? That is, if you can work a rehearsal into your busy schedule."

"What makes you say that?"

"I tried to call you last night. Your mom told me you were out."

"Speaking of being out, I just remembered something." Reaching into her white leather hobo bag, she grabbed her wallet. Inside was Lloyd's check. She held it open so Dean could read it for himself.

"Two hundred and fifty dollars, huh?" He kept reading. "Lloyd Newby."

"Remember him?"

Dean thought for a minute. "Is that the loser who stuck you with the tab at the French place?"

"One and the same." She pulled the check in each direction, resulting in a satisfying crackle of paper. "He paid me back, just like he promised." Joelle returned the check to its place in her red wallet.

Dean shrugged. "All right. You win. I'm happy for you. I know you're glad he finally repaid you. That's an awful lot of money to throw to the wind."

"It's all mine now. That check will be deposited in my bank account tomorrow." Joelle patted the outside of her bag as if putting the check to sleep for the night.

Dean tapped his fingers against his half-empty coffee mug. "Does this mean Mr. Lloyd Newby will be getting a second chance?"

Joelle couldn't believe her heart lurched when he asked. "Does it matter?"

"Just wondering. It's your life." He averted his eyes, and his voice took on a tone that convinced her he wasn't telling her the whole truth.

"If you really want to know, he hasn't asked me out again."

"Oh." He looked a little too pleased to suit Joelle. "If he did, would you go?"

She paused for effect but shook her head. "Not unless I had a lot of cash with me."

"Good. I think he was looking for a woman to foot his bills. From what you said, he seemed to enjoy the things money can buy." Dean drained his coffee cup. "Wonder what poor woman is paying his way now?"

"Woman? Why would you say that? It's his name on the check."

"So what? A girlfriend could have deposited the money in his account."

"I guess that's possible, but do you really think that's true?" The thought of taking another woman's money upset Joelle. She would rather not be paid back at all.

"I don't know, but if I were you, I'd deposit it as soon as possible." His voice took on an admonishing tone. "Just in case."

At that moment, the waitress interrupted them to offer refills on their coffee. After they both declined, she placed the check on the table.

"So," he said as he picked up the tab, "you never did tell me where you were last night."

"You never did tell me why you were calling."

He seemed as though he was about to say something when he thought better of it and changed his mind. "Tell you what. You leave the tip, and we'll call the whole thing even."

As they left, Dean promised to see her in church the next day. Only after Joelle got into her car did she realize that he hadn't offered her a lift to the worship service, as was his habit. For the first time in their long relationship, an uneasy emotion swept over her. She didn't like the feeling one bit.

CHAPTER 13

On Sunday afternoon, after the dishes from lunch were washed and the leftover chicken stashed in the refrigerator for sandwiches later, Joelle retreated to her room. The past weeks had proven to be such a whirlwind, she hadn't taken the time she needed to be alone with her thoughts and with the Lord.

As she changed out of her mint green cotton dress and pearl jewelry and into a comfortable pink terry cloth short set, Joelle thought about the day. During morning worship, Dean sat with Mandy and her family as was his custom, and Joelle sat with her parents and extended family who attended their church.

As expected, Dean's solo went over well. The poignant silence that followed his rendition of "Our God Is an Awesome God" told Joelle that the worshipers understood that modern music can be reverent. If Joelle had had her druthers, she would have led them in a standing ovation. She'd never heard the song performed as a solo. Dean's heartfelt, skillfully executed guitar arrangement, along with his rich tenor, made the words and tune seem especially worshipful.

After Sunday school, she congratulated him on a great performance. They agreed they needed to set up a time to rehearse for their duet. Then he was whisked away by some of the other church members who wanted to give their compliments, too. As she watched Dean shyly accept the praise, Joelle found herself looking forward to their rehearsals.

If only one of the men she'd met through the personals had been remotely like Dean!

She returned to the present with a sigh, remembering her resolution to answer one last ad. Surely the next person she called would be Mr. Right. Sitting on the bed, she drew the latest edition of *Today's Southwest Virginian Christian Singles* out of her nightstand drawer. Even though she hadn't fallen in love at first sight with any of her blind dates, she knew the little paper was the best place to find her next prospect.

Joelle flipped over the latest edition of the circular so she could study the front cover. A woman with frizzy permed hair and no makeup to hide crow's-feet wrinkles around her eyes stared back at her. The article about her was entitled "Living Single and Loving It!" Joelle noted the irony in the publication's running personal ads. The people they chose to interview each week weren't what the world would consider glamourous. Tricks of the secular magazines, such as windblown hair, soft lighting, and skimpy clothing, were never used to grab a reader's attention.

The paper she held had to be the safest venue to meet new men. With the word "Christian" in the title, she doubted anyone who wasn't a believer would even bother to read the newspaper. She nodded to herself. Any personal ads in this magazine were most definitely placed by Christians, she told herself again, particularly ones who were willing to look beyond the surface and into a person's heart. Even though the Christian men she'd met so far weren't as perfect as she'd first imagined, they'd been easier to cope with than nonbelievers such as Dustin, the boyfriend she had before her life-changing encounter with Christ. When she had still been enmeshed in that relationship, Joelle had kept her focus on the good times. Now that she had escaped, she saw that Dustin and his simmering rage had brought her more conflict than joy.

She turned to the back of the magazine. In the few weeks she'd been searching for someone, the ads, which appeared under the title "Solomon's Song," had doubled in size. Joelle wondered if the number of mateless people was increasing or if more people were finding out about the magazine and taking out ads. She couldn't help noticing that more men placed ads than women. She speculated men were more daring, or maybe they feared less for their safety than their female counterparts. Whatever the reason, she couldn't complain. More personals from them meant a wider selection for her.

Skimming the entries under "Single Men," she noticed Lloyd's ad was still running. His entry reminded her to say a word of thanks to the Lord for the check. Perhaps Lloyd hadn't been a perfect Christian, but over the course of their evening together, Joelle could see that he believed in Christ. He just hadn't given over his whole trust to the Lord. Otherwise, his interest in material gain wouldn't have been all-consuming. During her prayer, a surge of guilt shot through her, filling her with so much remorse that she stopped praying in midsentence. In that instant, she was convicted with the knowledge that money had motivated her to answer Lloyd's ad. He had promised candlelight gourmet dinners and travel to exotic places. Hadn't she wanted those things?

She had to admit, she still wanted to travel. She still liked to eat well. But she resolved not to let these carnal desires motivate other life decisions — particularly ones as critical as committing to the man she would one day marry.

After a moment, she resumed her prayer, confessing her weakness. Then she thanked the Lord that He had used her date with Lloyd to show her one area where she needed to change. She petitioned that she would stay on a path that led away from love of material possessions and the pleasures money can buy, and into His arms. She prayed that Lloyd would also find happiness in fewer possessions and seek fulfillment in the Lord's love. She closed her prayer without much hope that Lloyd would change or that she would hear from him again.

Joelle took a moment to marvel at those whose walk in the faith was such that they took comfort in all outcomes and lived as though they brooked no doubt. She knew she had a long way to go before she reached that point. In the meantime, Joelle was comforted by the knowledge that the Lord would be patient with her.

Quickly she added a prayer for the women who answered Lloyd's ad. The fact she didn't know their identities didn't matter. The Lord knew all.

Out of curiosity, she looked for Dexter's ad. She couldn't find it among the listings. Joelle mused that either Dexter had convinced Bertha to discontinue the ad, or he had finally become engaged to his Anastasia. Joelle sent up a prayer for the couple. If God's plan was for Anastasia and Dexter to make a match, she hoped the union would be blessed. No matter what woman Dexter eventually married, she prayed his mother would accept her new daughter-in-law.

She felt a nudging about Wilbert. She prayed he, too, would find the right woman. After she closed her prayer, Joelle wondered if Wilbert would ever find a woman whose goal in life was a sparkling kitchen floor — not that maintaining a clean apartment would be an easy task with his brothers around. Perhaps finding a woman would be the best thing Wilbert could do. If he married, his brothers would be forced to move and make their own way. Even so, Wilbert had given her the impression his main objective in a relationship was to gain an errand girl and housekeeper. Joelle wasn't afraid of work, yet she wanted the man she chose to see her as more than a way to accomplish his chores.

Sighing, Joelle picked up her beloved white teddy bear. She placed the bear, which she had improbably christened with the elaborate name Theodosia, next to her chest. Hugging Theodosia, she curled her legs until her knees touched the bear's ears. Joelle wished she could return to a simpler time, a time when she was a little girl and her main concern was whether she'd be getting the latest Barbie for Christmas. Hugging her teddy bear made her feel almost as though that dream were possible.

Joelle could indulge such a fantasy in her present surroundings. The bedroom had not been redecorated since she was twelve. On her birthday that November, her parents had presented Joelle with her very own bedroom suite. The desk, dresser, vanity, and canopy bed were made of knotted wood. She could tell because even the thick coat of white paint didn't conceal the round and oval shapes of the dark knobs. Pink flowers were strategically stickered onto each piece as decoration. They matched the medium shade of pink that Dad had painted on her walls while she was at a sleepover. She found out later the slumber party had been arranged just so they could surprise her. That day lived on in Joelle's memory as one of the happiest she could remember. As a result, the room remained almost untouched, a souvenir of that day.

Though she was no longer that preteen girl, taking refuge in that room was like turning back the clock to a simpler time, when the decisions she had to make seemed much more important than they were. Even now, she could lean her back against the pink pillow shams that rested on the headboard. She could turn on her CD player and let the soothing sounds of her favorite artists flood the room. She could keep munching on the bag of cheese curls that she still wasn't supposed to be eating on her bed, despite the fact she was an adult and took care of her own laundry.

Retreating to her room, hugging Theodosia, listening to music, and feasting on forbidden cheese curls was what she'd always done whenever she had a problem or faced a dilemma. Usually, after contemplation, she could talk herself into doing what her parents wanted her to do, or what her friends thought she should do, or even what she thought was right.

She wondered what Dean would have

thought of Wilbert.

Joelle let out a groan. Why did Dean always have to interfere with every decision? Could she ever get away from worrying about what he would think?

Maybe not. Maybe that's why she hadn't told him she'd been out with Wilbert. Maybe Wilbert was a threat, whether Joelle had acknowledged it at that point or not. But Dean had no reason to feel threatened, especially now that he was seeing Nicole.

Her treacherous heart reacted by sending forth a flood of anxiety. Why hadn't Dean told her about Nicole? He looked like he was about to, but something stopped him. What?

"He knows I don't approve of Nicole. That's what it is," she grumbled. "What in the world made him ask her out, of all people? They have nothing in common except the singles' group. And she doesn't even seem halfway committed to that."

An unbidden thought occurred to her. Dean didn't have to ask her approval. Sure, they were friends, but that didn't give her the right to dictate who he should and shouldn't see. She had to realize that.

"Besides, he sure wouldn't approve of me trying the personals again." With a motion of rebellion, she snapped the paper open and began reading. "I'll show Dean Nichols who's right."

CHAPTER 14

Still reclined on her bed, Joelle set her teddy bear by her side and started combing through the ads in earnest. With every man trying to make himself sound like Prince Charming, the ads differed little from each other. Joelle almost felt as though using the old childhood rhyme "Eeny meeny, miny, moe" would be as reliable as giving each great thought.

"Maybe you can tell me which one to call, Theodosia," she told her teddy bear. The stuffed animal's brown eyes remained unseeing, her mouth, with its pink tongue sticking out to one side, remained silent. "How does this one sound?"

Joelle read aloud:

Handsome, physically fit male, 35, seeks attractive, physically fit female, 20–40, for fun and games. Must love to watch football, soccer, tennis, and baseball as much as I do. Must also be a worthy tennis opponent. If throwing a Super Bowl party for the gang is the highlight of your January, then I'm your man!

"Whoever answers that will be running a mile a minute," Joelle told Theodosia. She scanned more ads.

"Here's one. 'I love the glamour of Old Hollywood and spend most Saturday afternoons with a bag of popcorn and a soda, staring at the silver screen. How about you?' " Joelle shook her head. "Not sure I want a couch potato. Wonder how much buttered popcorn he's consumed in his life?" After rolling her eyes at the bear, Joelle sighed and kept reading. Some of the ads had been running for weeks. She thought better than to take a chance on any of those. None of the new ads looked appealing. "Maybe I've gotten too cynical, or maybe the Lord is trying to tell me to wait. What do you think?" Ready to give up, she folded the paper. Suddenly, her gaze rested on a new ad:

Sensitive, spiritual man, 29, in quest of sensitive, spiritual woman, 22–32, who is willing to explore the love of God. Fellow seekers wishing to follow a path of inquiry and discovery with the desire to develop a committed relationship are most appealing. If you judge only by the outside of a person, not his heart, or if material gain, status, and power are what you desire, look elsewhere. But if you want to experience Freedom, true Freedom, then call me.

She read the ad several times, concentrating on the meaning of each phrase. "Maybe that's it," she told her bear. "I've been saying I really wanted to focus on my spiritual growth. Since that's all this ad promises, maybe this man is worth meeting."

With hope in her heart, she reread the latest ad. Its author didn't reveal anything about his interests, other than the spiritual. Surely the Lord must be first and foremost in this man's life.

"That must have been my mistake," she mused. "I should have been looking for someone totally devoted to the Lord." She looked at the printed promises again. "He says he wants a fellow seeker. Hmm. I guess I qualify. What do you say, Theodosia? Do you think I should take the plunge?"

Speaking the words aloud gave her the courage she needed. Without thinking further, she picked up the phone and made the call. Expecting to wait through a few rings, Joelle was taken aback when a man answered almost before the first ring was complete.

"You must have been right beside the phone," she blurted.

"Yes, I was." The voice was guarded. "Do I know you?"

"No —"

"Look," the voice grew gruff, "if you're calling again about that newspaper subscription, I told you I'm not interested. Can't you people take no for an answer?"

"Don't hang up!" When she didn't hear the click of the receiver cutting off the connection, she continued. "I'm calling about the personals ad in *Today's Southwest Virginian Christian Singles.*"

"Oh! The ad!" The voice became softer. "I'm sorry I was rude. You sound just like the woman who keeps begging me to take out a newspaper subscription."

"So I gathered."

He snickered. "Can we start over?"

"Sure. Can't hurt." She paused for effect. "I'm calling about a personals ad in the latest edition of *Today's Southwest Virginian Christian Singles* — the one that promises freedom. Am I speaking to the man who placed it?"

"As a matter of fact, you are. It's nice to meet you."

"Nice to meet you, too." She giggled in spite of herself.

"So," he asked, "out of all the ads you must have read, what made you decide to call me?"

As a variety of responses flashed through her mind, she decided honesty was the best tactic. "I'm looking for someone spiritual."

"Good. Are you a spiritual seeker?"

"I'm always looking to draw closer to the Lord, yes."

He paused. Joelle wondered if he didn't like what she had to say. "Hello?" she asked. "Are you still there?"

"Yes, I'm still here." He didn't say more, allowing silence to ease over the phone line.

She hadn't expected her future date to be so shy. An adventurer was what she had pictured, since he'd advertised himself as a seeker. Joelle tried to bring him out of his shell. "So, what else would you like to tell me about yourself?"

"I have good intuition. I can tell just from talking to you that you are a very good person."

"I'm working on it." She let out a nervous giggle. "So what's your name?"

"The name my parents gave me is Abe,

but my real name is Freedom."

"Freedom." The name seemed strange, until she remembered the wording of his ad. "You sure were clever in your ad."

"I thought so."

"So why did you change your name?"

"I thought it suited me better than the name of a Jewish patriarch. When you meet me, I'm sure you'll agree."

Joelle found Freedom's objections confusing. "Are you Jewish?"

"Of course not," he scoffed. "If I were, I wouldn't have placed an ad in a magazine with 'Christian' in the title, would I?"

"I guess not." Joelle felt foolish — too foolish to ask him to confirm he was a Christian.

"So what's your name? I'm assuming you still use the one your parents chose for you."

"Of course. I'm Joelle."

"Joelle. Hmm." He paused.

"It's a combination of my parents' names," she found herself explaining.

"Charming. I'll bet you're a brunette."

Joelle smiled into the phone. "I'm afraid your intuition failed you this time. I'm a natural blond, although I do wear teal contacts to liven up the color of my eyes."

"Is that your only form of subterfuge?"

"I like to think so."

"Good. You sound like someone who's up for exploration," he said. "Meet me at the Towne Center Complex at seven o'clock this Friday night. You won't regret it."

"Wait! How will I know it's you?"

"You will. Trust me."

"Who were you just talking to, dear?" Her mother was cutting up leftover meat for the night's roast beef hash. "Your father told me you were on the phone."

She shrugged. "A guy I know. It's no big deal."

Eleanor's face looked hopeful. "Wilbert?"

"No. Someone else. Sorry to disappoint you."

"Well, as long as you're having a good time. You're only young once, and the decision you make as to whom to spend the rest of your time on Earth with is the most important one of your life. Besides accepting the Lord, that is." She placed the chopped meat in a container and handed it to Joelle with a wordless motion for her to find a place for it in the refrigerator. She swept the floor as Joelle moved dishes aside and slid the container of beef in between canned sodas and Jell-O.

"Have a cup of tea?" her mother offered.

"Not right now, thanks."

Joelle's mother took a seat at the kitchen table. "Talk for a minute, then?"

Joelle smiled. "Of course." She sat beside Eleanor. "You have a serious look on your face. Am I in trouble?"

"Anything but." Her mom chuckled. "I don't know if we ever told you this, Joelle, but your father and I are so proud of you."

"Proud of me?"

"For accepting the altar call this past fall and for trying to live a better life ever since."

"Thanks. Is the change that obvious?"

Eleanor laughed. "You're a lot more relaxed and pleasant to be around. Plus, I know you've been reading your Bible a lot more." She bent an eyebrow. "Not to mention, we have been seeing a parade of different men lately. I'm happy to say that none of them seems to be the least bit like Dustin."

"They're not like him at all, Mom. They're Christians."

"Quite a difference, isn't it?" Eleanor didn't wait for Joelle to answer. A knowing smile crossed her features. "I might as well tell you this. Ever since you accepted the Lord and broke off with Dustin, I've been praying that you'd find someone. Specifically, the man the Lord has in mind for you."

"Mom! It's not like I'm desperate!"

"A beautiful girl like you? You could never be desperate. It's just that I know you miss Dustin, even if he was awful to you."

"He wasn't so awful, really." Joelle averted her eyes all the same.

"Don't try to fool me. I know better. I also know enough about the world to realize that most of us women miss any relationship with a man, even a bad one, once it's gone. I don't want you going back to that. It's high time the Lord showed you the man He wants you to be with."

She lifted her face. "I can't say we disagree on that." Joelle nodded. "I've been praying about the new directions my life is taking, and I keep getting the strong feeling it's time to connect with the man I'll eventually marry. You know, I'd think with all the changes I'm making, bringing romance into the mix is the last thing anyone would suggest. Isn't that ironic?"

"The Lord's plans don't always seem to follow logic," her mother counseled. "And they certainly don't go by what makes sense by the standards of the world. You're wise to stay with how you think He's guiding you. I'll keep praying."

Ready to turn the conversation to a lighter vein, Joelle shook her head in mock derision. "So what's the matter? Are you tired of having me around?"

"Never. I dread the day you leave this house, but I get a sense that it's time. Accepting the altar call was the first step of the rest of your life. I can't pretend I understand why you and I both get the feeling the Lord's plans for you involve a man, but He knows best. I realize you turned down a lot of dates when you were committed to Dustin. I'm glad that's no longer the case."

Joelle tried not to cringe. She still didn't have the courage to tell her mother she was meeting men through the personals, even if they were in a Christian magazine. "I have to admit, it's been an adventure. You know how it used to be. I'd just hang out with a bunch of friends, and we'd all do things as a group. Dustin and I just drifted together." Joelle remembered their long courtship. "Other than the junior and senior proms, I'm not sure we even had what you'd call a real date."

"I'm not even sure I'd call that a date." Joelle's mother shook her head. "All that money I spent on those evening dresses, just so you could go to the prom for a half hour and then go to Dustin's and watch TV the rest of the night. What a waste."

"I know. All that fanfare and not much fun." She patted her mom on the shoulder. "I promise the next time I go to a prom, I'll buy my own dress."

"Thanks a lot." Eleanor chuckled. "Of course, the last thing your father and I want for you is to get back together with Dustin, but don't you miss some of your old girlfriends? I liked Tory and Nina."

Joelle allowed her lips to curl into a thin smile. The girlfriends she spoke of were good at putting on virtuous fronts but were out for nothing but trouble when no one else was around. Too interested in having a good time to settle down, they hadn't changed much since high school.

"Maybe you could invite them over sometime?"

"No, Mom. But thanks for the offer." Joelle had no desire to renew those friendships. "I don't have much in common with them anymore. If I called them or suggested we get together, they'd only try to convince me I should go back to Dustin. There's no way I could ever consider that. He was never honest with me."

"Then you're smart for not trying. You can never have a good, solid relationship with a man who's less than honest with you. That's one of the secrets to your father's and my marriage. We're always honest with each other." She smiled. "Although we do try to be tactful and not hurt each other's feelings."

A surge of guilt shot through Joelle. She knew someone she hadn't been honest with lately. That was the one thing that held their friendship together when all else seemed to fall apart. "I just remembered, Mom. I have a phone call to make."

Ignoring her mother's quizzical look, Joelle made a beeline for the privacy of her room. She dialed Dean's number from memory, her heart beating rapidly all the while.

The line was busy.

Who could he be talking to?

CHAPTER 15

Running his fingers through still-wet hair, a newly showered Dean plopped into the easy chair in front of the TV. Years ago, his mother had bought the chair by redeeming a large number of S & H Green Stamps. He had affectionately dubbed the chair "The Throne." As far as Dean knew, Green Stamps were a relic of the past, much like the turquoise vinyl of The Throne's original upholstery. The vinyl, which had been chilly in winter and stuck to his legs in hot weather, was now covered by a heavy-duty, knotty brown fabric that reminded Dean of indoor-outdoor carpet, except that it was slightly less scratchy.

His parents had replaced their living room furniture with a matching couch and chair in medium blue with a floral pattern. Mandy had asked for their couch, and Dean had gladly taken the cast-off chair. So what if it didn't match the green sofa he'd bought on sale when a local furniture dealer went out of business? Later, he sprang for lamps with floral shades that had appeared as though they'd be perfect counterparts for the sofa. Only after he got home and discovered they looked too minty did he realize the lamps were a final sale and he couldn't take them back. No wonder they'd only cost forty dollars each, when they were originally marked two hundred dollars. Figuring that's what he got for being greedy, he set the lamps on two inexpensive end tables he'd spent a weekend assembling. As for the lamps, he resolved to be thankful for the light they cast.

At that moment, the sun broke through the clouds, shining unforgiving light through the picture window. His attention momentarily drawn to the window, Dean could almost count the squares in the loosely woven blue-and-green draperies, obviously a product of a discount store, that the landlord had left as part of the decor. The transparent curtains almost matched the teal blue walls.

In the meantime, Dean tried to ignore the fact that his living room looked like the revenge of a scorned interior decorator. He hoped one day his future wife would take pride in outfitting a house they could call their own. For now, the hodgepodge of furniture he owned was good enough for a bachelor.

Dean pulled up the footrest of the knotty brown chair and settled into comfort. He deserved to rest. His three-mile run had been a good one. No one else had been running or walking on the track today. Without distractions of other joggers, he was able to think of nothing for awhile, letting his mind go blank except for keeping count of how many laps hc completed. Hiding behind thin cloud cover, the sun didn't beat down upon his back with any intensity. His moving legs stirred the air enough to keep him from overheating. Only after he stopped was Dean aware of how much he'd been sweating.

Now smelling of soap and deodorant and wearing athletic shorts and a T-shirt, Dean gulped a tall glass of cool water. He mindlessly pushed the buttons on the TV remote. Baseball season, a time when he pitched on Sunday afternoons for the church team, was over. Autumn's volleyball season had not yet begun. The Sunday night Bible study for young adults would resume soon, meaning Dean could fill empty Sunday afternoons preparing for the class.

In the meantime, the hours stretched out

endlessly before him, an unwelcome break from his business. He knew it was wrong to feel that way. The Sabbath was a gift from the Lord. A time to renew and replenish oneself. A time to rest so facing the work-week would be less tiring. Dean somehow felt Sunday afternoons shouldn't be spent alone.

At least Zach had called and let him know how things were going with Eagle and Raven. As expected, Eagle had been sullen as he boarded the plane and made no secret of his desire to return to the West Coast.

Zach had been more optimistic about Raven. He had asked Zach a few questions about his own faith and how it affected his life. Dean was grateful to hear those encour-aging words.

Dean was about to suggest to Zach that they get together for a pickup game of basketball at the school gym when his friend mentioned he had a full afternoon ahead of him catching up on work. After Zach hung up, Dean felt lonelier than ever.

If only he could make up some excuse to call Joelle. A year ago, he would have thought nothing of picking up the phone and asking her to share a malt with him at one of the local haunts. Though she'd usu-ally be groggy from her Saturday night adventures, she never turned him down, but things had changed. She had made it clear she was looking for a man to share her life with. Why else would she persist in looking through the personals?

Dean had been keeping Joelle in his prayers all his life, but he had been especially vigilant since she accepted Christ. In his heart, he knew he had always loved her. When he first came to that realization, they were in high school. Dean remembered feeling jealous that Joelle was becoming too attached to Dustin. He tried to convince himself his concern was only that of a close friend. No one could deny Dustin was a bad influence, yet Dean knew he really wanted Joelle for himself.

He had spent time alone in his room, praying about whether or not to speak up and make his feelings known to her. No matter how much he argued with God, His answer had clearly been "no." Even Joelle's steady church attendance wasn't enough. She freely admitted to him that she went mainly to appease her parents. Otherwise, Joelle hadn't bothered to put on a show of living a life pleasing to the Lord. The pain in Dean's heart was great. Going against the Lord to pursue an unequally yoked relationship would have been wrong. At best, a brief romance would have cost their friendship. At worst, Joelle would have influenced him to take up some of her bad habits. Then they both would have been swimming upstream to get out of Satan's snare — if they ever could.

In the meantime, Dean was grateful that the Lord hadn't led him to dissolve their friendship. Sometimes being Joelle's friend was agonizing. Each time Dustin got in trouble with his parents, the law, or both, she came crying to him. Each time Dustin betrayed her, Joelle would ask Dean's advice, only to abandon it as soon as Dustin pleaded with her to forgive him. When people Joelle called "friends" abandoned her, Dean's shoulder was there for her to shed her tears. Not once did Dean let Joelle down. Not even now, when she had gotten it in her head that she should go off on a wild goose chase, looking through a circular for dates.

He felt just as helpless now as he did back in high school. Joelle said she felt led to find a Christian man to share her life with. Dean knew he could be that man. Yet he couldn't bring himself to admit it to Joelle. Not only was Dean reluctant to speak up because she was so new to the faith, the real, living faith just within her grasp, but the minute he declared his love for her, a perfectly wonderful friendship could be ruined. But if he didn't, he would never know how much more he — or, rather, both of them — could gain.

The thought of mentioning his feelings to Joelle left him with an inexplicable feeling of nervousness. He knew he just wasn't ready. At least not yet. His prayers didn't give him a strong leading to share his feelings, at least not for the time being. Dean knew the time would come when the Lord, not he, saw fit.

Clearly, Joelle wasn't ready. Dean wondered where she had been on Friday evening when he had wanted to take her to the play. He almost wished Earl hadn't given him those tickets. Then he never would have found out that Joelle wasn't sitting at home, as lonely and dateless as he was.

And he wouldn't have resorted to calling Nicole.

What had he been thinking? Dean mentally kicked himself for being so naïve. He thought she realized he made the offer as one Christian friend to another. That idea flew out the window from the moment he arrived at her apartment to pick her up. If he didn't get the message from her heavy makeup and teased hair, the skintight Lycra shirt and painted-on blue jeans she wore, she made sure he couldn't mistake the impact she was trying to make from the moment she got in his car. He remembered his nervousness when she slid toward him, positioning herself squarely in front of the radio. Warning her that they could be ticketed for her failure to wear a seat belt didn't work. She simply dug down into the cracks of the seat and retrieved the middle lap belt, a device that was really meant for use only when the car was fully loaded with six passengers.

During the drive, she leaned toward him, making sure her spicy cologne wafted his way. She would have been disappointed if she had known the scent only made him realize how much he preferred Joelle's perfume. Nicole's eagerness to carry on conversations and the light touches she'd place on his shoulders or wrists when she spoke to him weren't unusual. They were signaling she wanted to be closer friends.

Why hadn't he seen that?

In hindsight, Dean saw that Nicole flirted with everyone. She wasn't above doing almost anything to get Zach's attention, despite Ashlynn's obvious interest in him. Nicole's voice purred when she spoke to Dean, but it took on the same quality when she spoke to anyone of the male persuasion — from eighteen to eighty.

Dean should have known Nicole wasn't really interested in seeing the play. He wondered why she agreed to go out with him at all. She certainly hadn't been interested in serious conversation, at least, not about anything that mattered. As they drove the fifty miles to the theater, Dean found himself wishing the drive were quicker. Her conversation tended toward secular music groups, R-rated movies, and some of the more unsavory television programs on the air — shows on premium cable channels he didn't even subscribe to, precisely because he knew the type of lurid fare they ran.

Nicole had been surprised that Dean had no idea what she was talking about when she broached those subjects. He was lost when she tried to explain television soap opera plots, and the names of the bands she listened to left him blank. As soon as she ran out of subjects, her frustration was evident.

"I can't believe it when you say you don't know what I'm talking about," she had said.

"Sorry, but I don't." Dean had made a show of keeping his eyes on the road. He didn't want to face her icy stare.

"I don't know why you think it's such a

big deal to watch TV. Everyone I know watches those shows, and everyone listens to the same music I do," she protested.

"Not everyone. I doubt anyone else at the singles' group does."

"Wanna bet?"

Dean wondered who among them she meant. He decided it best not to ask. "Now you know someone who doesn't." He smiled, hoping his levity would cheer her up.

"I don't believe it." Suddenly, she cast him an understanding look. Placing a delicate, manicured hand on his sleeve, she leaned close enough that he could smell the strong scent she wore. "Look, if you're afraid I'm going to tell anyone at the singles' group that you actually watch TV, don't worry. I won't. Besides, I've already told you I do, so we'd both be in trouble, wouldn't we?" She sent him a sly little smile, as if they shared an intimate secret.

Dean wasn't sure what to say. If he protested that his lifestyle wasn't an act that he turned off and on to please different audiences, she'd probably accuse him of being a goody-two-shoes. If he pretended to agree, he'd be a liar. The more he thought, the longer the silence in the car lasted. Nicole had obviously figured out his answer without his saying a word. Moving toward her side of the car, she folded her arms across her chest and looked out her window.

"You think I'm immune to temptation, don't you?"

She turned her face in his direction. She was wearing a sneer. "You act like it."

"Well, I'm not. I'll give you one example. Not a month goes by that I don't get offers in the mail for cable television. Not just for the good stations, but for the ones that show what they call 'adult' programs, too. I have a confession to make. I should throw the ads away without even reading them, but sometimes I look at them anyway. I have to say, some of the pictures they show and the plot lines they describe are enough to make the pages sizzle."

Nicole let out a throaty laugh. "Then why don't you subscribe, just to see the programs you like? You're a big boy. It's your right to watch whatever you want. Besides, if you don't like a program, you can always switch the channel or discontinue the service. Since you live alone, no one will ever know."

"That's where you're wrong. I'll know, and God will know."

She arched a doubtful eyebrow. "Do you really think God will send down a bolt of lightning to punish you for hearing a cuss word?"

"No, but I don't think Jesus would want me to live my life that way."

"Your conscience is overactive. It's keeping you from living in the real world."

"Thank the good Lord for that!" he couldn't resist replying.

Nicole's expression didn't become more friendly, nor did she share his amusement. They spent the rest of the car ride in silence.

True to Nicole's observation, his conscience did become overwrought. Once again, he'd had a chance to witness . . . and once again, he had failed.

As he thought back to that night, the telephone rang.

"Dean?" The sexy purr was unmistakable.

"Nicole?"

"Surprised to hear from me, aren't you?" She let out a melodic chuckle.

"I must say, I am."

"First of all, I hope you can forgive me for last night. I didn't mean to skip out on my promise to do the lesson."

"That's okay. I muddled through. Although I must say, you missed out on some excitement with Zach's cousins." He went on to fill her in on the previous night's events.

"I wouldn't worry if I were you," she consoled. "I'm sure they'll both benefit from your influence. Speaking of influence, I have a favor to ask. Can I come over?"

CHAPTER 16

Several days later, Joelle sat at the computer in Dad's home office. She typed Dean's e-mail address and couldn't help but think of the irony of contacting him by computer when they lived only two miles apart. There seemed to be no other choice. After several unsuccessful attempts to reach him by phone on Sunday, she had given up and driven by his house, hoping he wouldn't notice. Worry was needless. His car was gone.

After work on Monday, she drove by his house again, only to see that the driveway was still empty. Phone calls to his home led to nothing but listening to his answering machine. His cell phone had been turned off. This afternoon was Tuesday, and the same pattern prevailed. E-mail seemed to be the only answer. After dashing off a quick note for him to contact her, Joelle pressed SEND and hoped for the best.

She hadn't even gotten up from her seat at the desk when the telephone rang.

She chuckled to herself. "That was quick!" Smiling, she picked up the receiver, ready to talk to Dean. "Hello?"

"Yes, hello." To Joelle's disappointment, her telephone caller was a female. "Is this Joelle?"

The voice was familiar, but she couldn't pinpoint the caller's identity. "Yes? This is she." The hesitation in her own voice was evident.

"This is Bertha."

For a split second, the name didn't register. Then she remembered. "Bertha!" Joelle wondered what possible reason Dexter's mother could have for calling. She only hoped it wasn't to arrange another date with her son. Unable to think of anything better to say, she uttered, "Good to hear from you."

"Good to talk to you again, too." Bertha's voice sounded as chipper as she remembered. "Is this a good time? You've already eaten supper, haven't you?"

"Yes." She consulted the clock. The time was 5:56. "Your timing is perfect. I got up from the table not ten minutes ago," Joelle assured her caller. Unenthusiastic about continuing with mindless chitchat, Joelle let silence permeate the line, hoping Bertha would get to the point. She didn't mind that Bertha had called. The older woman was charming enough. Still, considering Dexter's and Bertha's opposite opinions about his girlfriend, Joelle knew any further involvement on her part would only place her in the middle of a family war.

"So how are you doing?"

"Fine, thanks." Joelle tapped her foot.

"Any luck with the personal ads?"

Joelle decided on a truthful answer that she hoped gave enough information to deter Bertha's plans for her to see Dexter again, assuming that was the reason for her call. "I met someone else."

"Oh." Joelle could visualize Bertha's crestfallen expression.

Feeling a rush of guilt, Joelle added, "But I can't say I've been swept off my feet by any of the other men I've met through the personals."

"Oh!" Her voice sounded hopeful. "In that case, I'm calling to invite you on a fabulous trip!" Bertha was saying her words at a fast clip, her excitement unmistakable. "How does Las Vegas sound?"

"Las Vegas?" No way could Bertha have an inkling as to how significant Las Vegas was to Joelle.

She and Dustin had talked many times of eloping to Sin City. How many times had they seen its lights on television and in the movies? Blinking and running lights that looked so fascinating on film had to be even better up close and in person. Fabulous hotels, all meant to recreate the wealthy life-styles of times past, looked bigger and better than any place Joelle had ever seen, much less stayed at as a guest. Spinning black and red wheels, men and women card dealers dressed in black-and-white tuxedos, a sea of machines, all ready to take — and give back — money; all looked appealing to a young woman who'd seldom had reason to leave her home in the mountains.

If the prospect of seeing such man-made wonder wasn't enough to lure the adventurous young couple, the city's reputedly lax attitude and promise of a wedding chapel on every corner sealed the deal. Their shared secret plans, usually whispered when Dustin knew Joelle was miffed with him, seemed at the time to draw them closer. Only recently had Joelle come to the realization that Dustin had merely dangled the prospect in front of her, stringing her along. His failure to keep his vow made Joelle feel as though she were the one who had failed. Only now could she be thankful that Dustin had never kept his promise to marry her in Las Vegas or anywhere else.

Joelle no longer had any desire to visit the city. Especially not with Dexter and his mother.

Bertha broke into her thoughts. "I guess you're wondering how I could afford to offer you such a wonderful vacation. Can you believe I won it? I never win anything. I just filled out a sweepstakes form on impulse. You know, one of those solicitations that comes in the mail? I seem to have gotten on all the lists of people who like to try for prizes. Guess a little birdie at Bingo must have tipped them off." She giggled. "Anyway, the trip is for two! Isn't that exciting?"

Unwilling to obligate herself to Bertha, Joelle searched for something graceful to say. "I'm flattered that you thought of me, but I would have assumed Dexter would be your first choice as a traveling companion."

"Oh, he's going, too!"

"I thought you said the trip is for two."

"It is! But since we will be going for free, I can pay your way. What do you say?"

Joelle didn't answer right away.

"I can't believe you're not jumping at a chance for a free trip to somewhere so exotic." Bertha sounded hurt.

"I know. It sounds lovely, but —" Joelle

searched for an excuse. "I might not have the vacation time, and I don't gamble. That's the main attraction at Vegas, isn't it?"

Bertha chuckled. "For an old lady like me, maybe. But there are a lot of other things to do. You can see Hoover Dam, and there are lots of shows." Bertha took in a breath. "Oh, I almost forgot. They included tickets to a rock concert. I've forgotten the names of the people who are scheduled to play. I haven't kept up with that sort of thing since the Beatles broke up. Let me get my glasses so I can read the tickets. Hold on."

The receiver clunked, presumably on a table, while Bertha searched for her eyewear. Joelle heard rustling noises, then the sound of footsteps clacking this way, then that. Bertha seemed to be having trouble finding her glasses. Still sitting at the computer, Joelle was tempted to begin a game of Freecell. She had just begun to call up the program when Bertha returned to the phone.

"Here they are. Do you know any of these groups?" Bertha named three rock groups that had been Joelle's favorites when her relationship with Dustin was hitting its stride.

"Yes, I know them," she admitted.

"Great! Wouldn't you like to go to the concert?"

Joelle swallowed. She didn't want to admit she'd always wanted to see every group Bertha named but had never gotten a chance.

"You don't have to tell me. I know you'd love to go."

"But —"

"You don't have to give me a firm answer right away. Why don't you sleep on it and give me a call later in the week? It'll be so much fun! That much I can promise." Bertha's delight was such that Joelle could almost hear her smile. Painful as the situation was, Joelle knew she had to be firm. "I can tell you right now, Bertha. My answer is no. I'm really sorry, but I just can't go."

"Are you sure?"

"Positive."

Bertha mumbled something polite and quickly excused herself. Joelle felt sorry for her. As she hung up, Joelle wondered if perhaps seeing some of the shows would be nice, and to go somewhere touted in the movies would be a novelty. Most likely, she would never have another chance to visit Las Vegas, at least not in the foreseeable future. Yet even if she were an avid gambler, going on the trip would unfairly encourage

Bertha, and it certainly wouldn't be fair to keep stringing along Dexter.

Why did the wrong men always chase her? Or at least, the wrong man's mother? At the thought, she laughed in spite of herself. Being courted by a man's mother on her son's behalf was a first.

Not that being with Dexter was worse than death itself. He seemed decent enough. Maybe he'd liven up and actually enjoy a rock concert.

A rock concert. She sighed. A year ago, she would have packed her bags as soon as Bertha mentioned the concert. The prospect of hearing and seeing the performers extol one-night stands, whiskey, even drugs, to catchy tunes would have been too hard to resist. Self-indulgent lyrics encouraged listeners to look out for their own interests and pleasures, to credit themselves with any success they had in life, and to grab every carnal opportunity. Joelle knew the lifestyle they espoused wasn't moral. It certainly wasn't the one her parents would have chosen for her. Yet only a few months ago she would have argued that there was no harm in enjoying the tunes as long as she didn't try to follow their suggestions too closely. The desire to stay healthy had kept Joelle from indulging as the singers suggested. So did the casual, intellectual relationship she had with the Lord at the time.

Now she realized she had to go beyond simply not acting upon every suggestion. Now that she sought a personal relationship with Christ, Joelle realized how wrong it would be to attend a concert that did nothing to honor the Lord.

Okay, maybe it is wrong, a voice inside her head argued, *but no one will ever know. Well, no one except Dexter and Bertha. And who'd ask them?*

Dean would find out, her conscience argued.

Not if you don't tell him, the voice insisted. *Besides, who cares what he thinks? He left town and didn't even bother to leave a number with you.*

The more she considered how Dean was neglecting her, the more her ire rose. Joelle let out a ragged breath and narrowed her eyes. Unwilling to debate with herself any longer, Joelle scanned the nearby bookshelf. A few of her old compact discs were still in the place where she had abandoned them months ago. Pulling out one of her former favorites, she slipped it into the computer tower and set the audio function to play the best song. Pounding drums and wailing guitars were her reward.

Joelle signed back on to the World Wide Web. She had to see if Dean had returned her e-mail. By the time she discovered there was still no message, the singer was boasting about his latest conquest. Somehow, the songs didn't seem fun anymore.

CHAPTER 17

"I can't believe how out of shape I am!" Joelle groaned as she stepped into the shower a few nights later. Every muscle in her legs felt tight from doing over a hundred walking lunges during class. Both arms were limp from a heavy-duty session of lifting free weights. Even five pounds felt like too much by the third set. Joelle shuddered at the memory.

She had stopped by the high school gym on the way home from work. Fawn, an old classmate, had just become a certified aerobics instructor and was offering new classes. The previous week, Fawn had dropped by the doctor's office where Joelle worked, class list in hand. She prodded Joelle to take a class. Joelle had agreed, wanting to help out an old acquaintance and feeling confident that an hour-long class would prove effortless.

After the first twenty minutes, Joelle had

barely broken a sweat and her breathing wasn't labored. As the class progressed, however, the exercises and dance moves increased in complexity and intensity. Forty minutes into the hour, she was huffing and puffing. The neck of her athletic shirt was drenched. Joelle's glance fell on the clock every few seconds. She hoped the next twenty minutes would move fast. If they didn't, Joelle was tempted to quit. Mercifully, after fifteen more minutes of agony, the class moved into the five-minute stretch and cool down. She hadn't remembered a time in the recent past when she'd been so glad to see the end of an hour.

Once in the shower, Joelle was grateful to feel streams of water pounding all over her body. As steam rose into her nostrils, her thoughts returned to Dean. At least the class had taken her mind off of him and why he still hadn't called. She couldn't recollect the last time four days had passed without them speaking to each other. Over the past week, Joelle realized for the first time how much she depended on his companionship, and how much she missed him when he wasn't there.

Sweat washed away by moisturizing soap and warm water, Joelle jumped out of the shower, toweled dry, and applied scented lotion. After retrieving her comfy, white terry cloth robe from the hook, she wrapped it around herself. Never mind that the weather outside was hot. In her air-conditioned bedroom, she enjoyed the comfortable feeling of being safe and snug inside the cozy garment.

Sitting at her vanity dresser, Joelle had just plugged in her hair dryer when the buzzing telephone demanded to be answered. She ran to the nightstand and picked up the receiver, hoping to hear a familiar baritone. "Hello?"

"Joelle?"

Her shoulders sagged with relief. "Dean! Where were you? I've been trying to get you all week."

"So I saw on my caller ID."

"Oh." Joelle felt her cheeks flush. She'd forgotten he could tell the number of attempts a caller had made, even if the person didn't leave a message. How many times had she tried to reach him during the past week? Chagrined, she didn't even want to think about it. "I guess I thought if I tried enough times, I'd eventually get an answer."

"Apparently." He chuckled, as though he were accommodating a precocious young girl rather than being cruel or teasing. "I

226

was at the men's prayer and fasting retreat, remember? I told you about it at least a month ago."

Groaning, she tapped her hand against her forehead. "Now I remember."

"So you were worried about me?" He sounded pleased.

"Okay, I admit it. I would have been really concerned, except I got an away notice in response to my e-mail message. You better be glad I did. Otherwise, I might have called the police." She tried to keep her tone light, but she was only half-joking.

"I'm glad you didn't resort to that. I'm sure the police have better things to do."

"I don't know. There's so little crime around here, they might like a little excitement." Joelle plopped down on her bed. "The main thing is, you're home now. So how was the retreat?"

"Great. Men from all over the mid-Atlantic region attended. I saw a couple of people from last year. Remember I told you about Brock? His wife had a baby."

"Good. You had said he was concerned about the pregnancy. I'm glad everything turned out all right."

"So am I."

Even though Joelle couldn't have picked Brock out of a lineup of two men, the idea of a new life held genuine appeal. "So what was it?"

"What was what?" Dean paused, presumably to think. "Oh, you mean the baby? I don't know. Hopefully it was either a boy or a girl." He let out a little laugh.

"Oh, I get it. You couldn't tell by the name, and you were too embarrassed to ask. What was it? Let me guess." Joelle pursed her lips as she thought. "Sam? Alex? Lee?"

Dean hesitated. "Uh, I don't know what they named it."

"You were with him the whole week, and you don't even know if he had a boy or a girl, or what its name is, or anything?" Joelle's mouth was hanging open. "How can that be possible?"

"Um, I don't know."

"Men! They never find out anything." Joelle grimaced, even though Dean couldn't see her mock disgust. Giving up hope, she changed the subject. "So have you been home long?"

"Not too long. I would have called as soon as I got here, but I knew you were traveling in between work and home."

"Not to mention I stopped by the gym and took a new cardio class. Remember Fawn, from high school? She's teaching them now."

"Fawn Fields?"

"Fawn Johnson now. She married somebody from Maryland."

"She was in algebra with me, but other than that, I didn't know her. But you and I must be on the same wavelength. I got back from my run a few minutes ago and took a quick shower before I called. I'm willing to bet we both have wet hair." He chuckled.

"You'd be right." Joelle twisted a lock of dripping hair around her finger. "You're a bundle of energy. I can't imagine driving two hundred miles, then immediately going to the track."

"To tell the truth, I missed running. They didn't budget any time for exercise, and I was ready to get my legs moving again."

"Even on an empty stomach?"

"We broke the fast with a simple dinner, so I can't really say I was starving when I left the retreat. I'd be lying if I didn't confess that I stopped at the first fast-food place I saw and ordered a double cheeseburger and large bag of fries." Joelle could imagine him grinning into the phone. "Fasting was definitely my least favorite part of the retreat."

"I don't think I'd be enthusiastic about it, either," she admitted.

"So now you know what I've been up to.

229

What about you? I know you must have had some reason for calling a hundred times. What did you want to talk about?"

"Nothing. And everything." She let out a sigh. "I have something to tell you. It's about these guys I've been meeting through the personals."

"Oh." His utterance was devoid of expression, and he didn't elaborate. The silence was heavy with anticipation.

Though Joelle had set out to tell him everything right then, suddenly spilling over the telephone didn't feel right. "Dean," she asked aloud, "can I come over?"

"Umm —"

"Oh, I know what it is. You want to dry your hair." Her tone was teasing. "Don't worry, I'll give you plenty of lead time to get all gussied up. Even if it is just little ol' me."

He chuckled, but it sounded forced. "Uh, this isn't exactly the best time."

"It's not? Are you okay?"

"Yeah. Yeah, I'm fine. It's just that —" he interrupted himself. "It's just that, I promised I'd meet someone at the diner, that's all."

Joelle felt her heart leap into her throat. Her stomach did a funny backflip. It wasn't a nice backflip, the kind she got when she was about to open a long-anticipated gift, or even the daredevil feeling of fright just as the hydraulic safety latches tied her into the seat right before a roller coaster ride. Instead, the feeling was one of disappointment, unwelcome surprise, and —

No. It couldn't be.

Taking a mental breath, Joelle decided to keep her voice as light and coquettish as she could. "I don't suppose you're going to tell me who your mysterious compadre is, are you?"

He hesitated. She could visualize the wheels turning in his mind, debating whether or not to tell her. That wasn't a good sign. If he had dinner plans with Zach or any of his other male friends, the name would have instantly zipped off of Dean's lips. His meeting had to be with a female. Maybe a female who was more than a friend . . . or wanted to be more than a friend.

Joelle became conscious that her heart was beating faster than usual. She didn't speak. She waited for him to answer.

"It's Nicole."

Nicole. The very name she didn't want to hear.

"I see." A familiar rush of feeling swept over her, the kind of feeling she used to have whenever Dustin had been out without her and wouldn't tell her where, why, or with whom. She recognized that feeling.

It was jealousy.

"Just hope you enjoy your little visit." If she didn't end the call at once, Joelle knew she'd say something she'd later regret — probably for the rest of her life. She was just about to send him off with an abrupt farewell and hang up when he answered.

"What's that supposed to mean?" His voice was testy.

"Nothing. I'm sorry. As soon as I said that, I regretted it." A shocking realization came to her at that moment. One she did not embrace.

"That's okay, Joelle."

Dean was always so understanding. Too understanding, sometimes. Too willing to let her treat him like a favorite pair of blue jeans. Always reliable. Always dependable. Always the right fit. Always there. Always convenient.

But it looked like all that was about to change.

"Look, Dean," she said, "you don't owe me anything. You have your own life, and I understand that. I should have realized that long ago. You're entitled to see whoever you want, whenever you want. It's really none of my business. It's not like I have a claim on you. I'm sorry."

"No problem. Thanks for the apology."

Joelle hung up the receiver slowly, letting it barely touch the cradle before gently releasing it to its proper place. She ran her finger up and down the receiver, but she wasn't thinking about the object. She was thinking of Dean. For a man who'd just gotten her to apologize, he hadn't sounded happy. Not happy at all.

"I was wondering where you were," her mom called as Joelle passed the master bedroom some time later.

Responding, Joelle detoured into the room. Eleanor was standing in front of the full-length mirror, spritzing her blond hair with spray. "I wanted to let you know, your dad and I are going out with the Martins for dinner. You're on your own tonight, kiddo."

Joelle let out a low whistle. "I could have guessed. That dress looks great on you, Mom."

Casting her gaze downward, Eleanor appraised herself, then twirled 360 degrees for Joelle to see. "You think?"

"Sure do. Royal blue has always been your color."

"I hope so. We're trying that French place

Lloyd took you to. I know it's pretty nice. The Martins said they wanted to treat us because I finally got up enough courage to take the GED test." Her mother's face took on a pink hue, a sure sign she was embarrassed to mention her accomplishment.

Joelle remembered the party that was being planned to celebrate. She couldn't let on, since she'd been sworn to secrecy. "You deserve to go out to a fancy place and much more."

"I don't know." She smiled shyly, reminding Joelle of how she looked in pictures taken decades before. "So how was the exercise class? Will you be going back?"

"Probably." Joelle grinned. "I always was a glutton for punishment."

Eleanor chuckled. "Oh, before I forget, you got some mail today. I have no idea why your father brought it in here. I just happened to see it, thankfully, or else we might not have paid the electric bill. He never bothers to sort it." Shaking her head, she picked up a stack from a tray on top of their television and handed it to Joelle.

"Thanks." Absently, she riffled through catalogs, charge card offers, advertisements, and letters. Stopping at her bank statement, she opened it, even though she had no intention of balancing her checkbook until after dinner.

"Who was that on the phone?"

"Dean."

"Oh, good. So where was he? I know you were wondering."

"The men's retreat. I'd forgotten all about it."

"So had I," said Eleanor, before launching into a story of a mishap that had occurred to Joelle's father and his friends on a golf retreat.

Joelle wasn't listening to her mother. She was too astounded by what her bank statement revealed. "I can't believe this."

"Can't believe what?" Eleanor interrupted herself. She placed her hands on her hips. "You weren't listening to a thing I said, were you?"

"I'm sorry. I guess I wasn't. It's just that, well, you won't believe this." Joelle wasn't sure she believed it herself. "Lloyd's check bounced. His bank returned it because of insufficient funds. And if that's not bad enough, our bank charged me twenty-five dollars."

"That's awful, Joelle. That bad check didn't cause you to overdraw your account, did it?"

"No, though that's no thanks to Lloyd." She sighed. "I just can't believe it. All this time, I thought he really was trying to make things up to me. I just ended up looking like a fool again. How stupid am I?" Her mouth drooped. "Don't answer that."

Eleanor chuckled. "You're not stupid. He fooled me, too."

Joelle grimaced. She had rubbed what she thought was a victory in Dean's face. He'd been right about Lloyd all along. "I guess I owe Dean another apology."

"You seem like you have a lot to talk to him about lately." Eleanor's eyes took on a knowing look. She seemed to be ready to make another comment but shut her mouth in a tight line, as though she thought better of it.

"Have a good time tonight, Mom," Joelle said. She hoped her voice showed the proper measure of enthusiasm.

Exiting the bedroom, she retreated to the kitchen to scrounge around in the refrigerator for supper. Not that she looked forward to eating.

All she could think about was Dean. And what he was doing with Nicole.

CHAPTER 18

Joelle was nervous as she drove to the next town. Consisting of two large department stores and a few small retailers, the shopping area where she and Freedom had agreed to meet was hardly what could be called a regional mall, yet the variety of merchandise offered was enough to satisfy the basic needs of most people in the surrounding communities. The theater and food court provided places for teens to meet and greet, and for families to get away for a relatively inexpensive evening out. Although he had made no such promise, Joelle assumed Freedom planned for the two of them to take in a movie after a light supper.

Finding a convenient parking place in the crowded lot wasn't easy. The cinema ran four movies at once, so the lot tended to fill up and stay full. Since it was Friday night, Joelle didn't bother to circle her car around the lot containing the closest spaces. The search would no doubt prove futile.

Anticipating her presence at the Silver Screen Matinee within the hour, Joelle didn't begrudge her fellow movie lovers their spaces. She didn't even care what movies were showing. Joelle was content to watch any of them. Against her will, she remembered several occasions when she and Dean had shared an afternoon and a bag of popcorn as they watched flickering black-and-white images. She hoped Freedom liked old movies, too.

Joelle pulled into a space in the far lot meant for an anchor store, making sure she parked beneath a light pole. Since darkness would be upon her by the time she left, she wanted to be sure her car was located in the safest place possible.

Unsure as to how her date would be dressed, Joelle had opted for the same outfit that had taken her to the French restaurant — casual slacks and a blouse, with flat shoes she knew would be comfortable. Being able to wear the same outfit several times had proven the only advantage to a series of blind dates. One change was evident — she had styled her grown-out hair into a flip that managed to look updated while sparing her the messy look.

As her steps took her closer to the entrance, she looked for Freedom. He had promised he'd be easy to spot. She wondered what he meant until she saw a tall, carrot-topped man in his twenties. He reminded her of Howdy Doody except that he was dressed in solid white. White shirt, white pants, white socks, white shoes. Since he was the most distinctive figure in the crowd, he had to be Freedom. She drew closer, still nervous.

He made eye contact. "You must be Joelle."

"I am. But how could you tell?"

He arched red eyebrows. "We just made a rhyme." Freedom cleared his throat and lifted his hand, pointing his forefinger skyward as though he were a professor. "You must be Joelle. But how could you tell? Because you look like a belle I'd like to know well."

Joelle laughed out loud at his corny humor. "I don't think I've heard a poem that bad since kindergarten."

"What?" His tone was mocking. "Are you implying my poetry isn't good enough for Public Television?"

"It's not even good enough for cable access. Sorry." She chuckled, shaking her head all the while. "So how did you know it was me? What really tipped you off?"

"You were scoping out the place like you were looking for somebody, so I took a guess."

"Well, you guessed right." She smiled. Though he was dressed in a somewhat unorthodox fashion, Freedom seemed harmless enough. "So what are your plans?"

"Hungry?"

"As a matter of fact, I could use a bite to eat." She hoped he'd suggest eating at the mall's midpriced restaurant since it offered a bit of atmosphere and a degree of privacy in comparison to the open layout of the food court.

Instead, he tilted his head toward one of the nearby booths, Very Veggie. "I like their organic pita sandwiches. Don't you?"

Since Joelle preferred to indulge in hamburgers and fries, Very Veggie was one of the places in the food court Joelle made every effort to avoid. "Uh, I've never tried one."

He seemed surprised. "As they say, there's a first time for everything. How does a BLT sound?"

Bacon, lettuce, and tomato sandwiches were a rare indulgence for Joelle. Yet at that moment, the prospect of salt and fat seemed comforting. "Sounds good."

"Why don't you go grab us a table, and

240

I'll bring you back a treat?"

Joelle wasn't sure she liked this idea, but she decided to acquiesce. Watching him walk toward the booth, she noticed he was carrying a tan leather briefcase. She wondered about its contents. Had he come straight from work to the date? If he had, he could have left the briefcase in his car. Unless he took a bus from his office to the mall.

But what makes you sure he works in an office? He never told you what he does for a living.

Joelle wished she'd asked more questions when they first spoke on the phone. Still, she brushed her worries aside. At least they were in a very public place. And, she reasoned, if the briefcase contained something sinister, he wouldn't be so open about carrying it.

Her thoughts running wild, she was thankful his order was filled quickly and he returned to the table as promised. She was considering whether to ask about the briefcase when he began the dinner.

"Here you go!" He handed her a sandwich. "I hope you like this. My wallet sure didn't." A nervous chuckle escaped his lips.

Joelle wondered if he was going to ask her to chip in, but since she had no say in the choice of restaurant or food, she decided not to extend her generosity. "I'm sure I'll like it."

"Very Veggie is a bit pricey, especially by food court standards, but I assure you, it's worth every penny."

"I'm sure." The smell the sandwich emitted was noxious. Trying not to make a face, at that moment she decided for certain there was no way she would pay for whatever it was he'd ordered for her. "What is it?"

"It's a BLT."

Joelle looked again. "This may have lettuce, but I don't see any tomatoes or bacon."

"That's right. This is a Beets, Lettuce, and Tofu sandwich. You'll see by its green color that the pita is spinach. They also use a scrumptious mustard-and-cider vinegar dressing. They're the only people who make this sandwich, and I make sure to get one every time I come here. Delicious! You'll be pleased to learn that all the vegetables are grown without harmful chemicals or any other artificial enhancements. They even make their own pitas and dressing." Beaming, he seemed pleased to present her with such a treat.

Organic or not, Joelle didn't think the combination sounded appealing. With an expectant glance at his sandwich, she inquired, "How about a trade?"

Freedom stared at the glass ceiling that loomed high above them. "Hmm. Let me think about that." After a moment he shrugged his shoulders and gave her a nod. "Okay. This is a sacrifice, but I'll trade just to show you I'm quite the gentleman." He handed her his sandwich.

"Thanks." She knew her relief was obvious, until a strangely familiar odor wafted to her nostrils. A quick look at her new sandwich confirmed her worst suspicions. "This is exactly the same."

"Precisely." A sheepish expression crossed his face. "Sorry you don't think you'll like it. Try it. You might be surprised." He placed a large drink next to her. "I got us both a banana sesame yogurt shake. I even splurged and bought us dessert." Freedom reached into a small bag and extracted a container with a transparent plastic lid. The cup contained an icy dessert that appeared to be orange sherbet.

"Looks yummy," she observed. This time she didn't have to control a grimace.

"It is! One of my favorites. Cantaloupe sorbet."

Joelle hoped she heard wrong. "What kind of sorbet?"

"Cantaloupe." Freedom looked at her as though she had just disembarked from a Venusian ship. "Never tried it?" He tapped his unopened straw on the lid. "You're in for a treat."

Joelle stared at the unappetizing meal. "Yum." She knew her expression and tone belied her approval.

Instead of noticing her facial cues, Freedom looked for the invisible. "I have a special talent for seeing auras. You know, very few people do." He bit into his pita.

Joelle was no longer accustomed to eating without pausing for a word of thanks. "You don't say a blessing before meals?" she asked. If any meal needed a blessing, it was this one.

He shook his head. "No. God is everywhere, in all of us. But if you feel the need to pray, I can respect that. I'll wait." Setting down his sandwich, he looked down at his lap.

Joelle bowed her head. "Lord, we gather to thank You for Your provision once again. Please be with us tonight, and bless our time together. In the holy name of Your Son, Jesus Christ, our Lord and Savior, amen."

Obviously untouched by her gesture, he picked up his food before the "amen" had left her lips. "Back to auras," he said. "I can tell by yours that you and I would make good companions."

"You can tell that just from seeing me for a few minutes?"

"Unequivocally. Through my spiritual exploration, I have gained the keys of knowledge." After taking a sip of his drink, he leaned forward. "Take, for example, your name. Joelle is not the name you were meant to have." He set down his sandwich and touched his fingers to his temples. "Give me a moment to release the energy in my mind and connect to your soul. Then I will see what you really should be called."

"I don't know. I like Joelle —"

He held up his hand. "Shh! I can't communicate without absolute silence."

Unable to think of a reason not to accommodate his request, offbeat though it was, Joelle decided to obey. She was glad for the excuse to stop nibbling on the portion of the spinach pita that had managed to escape a soaking from beet juice.

As Freedom closed his eyes and kept them closed for some time, she cast shy glances at those around her. They were ignored by most of the people milling about the mall, but others looked at them in wonderment. They even attracted a couple of snickers. Joelle tried to ignore them by sipping on the oddly flavored shake.

Finally, Freedom came out of his trance. "I just received a message about your new name." He opened his blue eyes. "It's Discover."

"Discover?" She wasn't sure she could get used to such an eccentric name. "You mean, like the credit card?"

"So you are overly concerned about wealth. If you weren't, you wouldn't have thought of a credit card when you heard that name. But don't worry," he consoled her. "Soon the name Discover will come to mean much more to you than a piece of plastic. You have so much to learn, so much to explore, so much to discover."

"I don't know —"

"Today's women are more free than they have been in any other time in history. I don't believe in keeping women in the shackles of old myths and ideas. That keeps me at liberty, too. I am free from all jealousy and can easily give you as much space as you give me. That way, we both can share our liberty." He leaned closer. "Are you free from the bonds of the world? Can you pick up and move anytime you like?"

"I don't know. My parents might be disappointed if I were to move out, except to get married, of course."

"You live with your parents?" His eyes widened. "You're not still in high school, are you?"

"Of course not. I work full time in a doctor's office."

"I hope she practices alternative medicine."

"It's a he, and no, he doesn't practice alternative medicine." This was not going well. Joelle began to wonder how she could finagle her way out of the rest of the evening.

Instead of delivering her the expected lecture on women's equality and the merits of alternative medicine, Freedom went off on another tangent. "Speaking of alternatives, I'm sure you've been speculating as to what I have in my briefcase."

Joelle was stunned. Just as she was about to cut him off, Freedom always managed to come up with something to intrigue her enough to stay put. "I'll have to admit, I was wondering."

Leaning over, he pulled the briefcase onto his lap, snapped it open, and drew out some pamphlets that appeared to be professionally printed. He smiled endearingly. "You never asked me where I live or about my career."

"I assumed you live within striking distance of here. As for what you do, I figured you'd tell me sooner or later."

"You are a very unusual woman, Joelle. Normally that's the first thing a woman wants to know. I'll let you in on something. The fact you didn't ask is one reason I knew you're special. You look beyond the money issue," he grinned, "even if you do think your new name is like a credit card."

"I've been working on my attitude about money. I guess what you said proves I still have a ways to go." She let out a sigh. "I only recently accepted Jesus Christ. He has a lot of molding left to do."

"Ah, Jesus Christ. A fine teacher much like Buddha. If you choose to embrace Jesus why not let Him mold you where you can truly be free? Where you can live out the potential of your new name?"

"I'm making plenty of discoveries where I am, thanks."

"Maybe. But look at how much better this place is." He handed her a pamphlet.

Joelle studied the picture depicting a quiet valley in full summer bloom. Mountains touched an azure sky. Just looking at it had a calming effect.

"How would you like to live there?"

"I already live in the mountains. I love it here. Maybe that's why I find this picture so appealing." She tried to return the pamphlet, but he refused to accept it.

"Read the inside."

The leaflet expanded into more full-color photos. Some showed smiling people working together at a pottery wheel. A crowd of happy children played in another. Two large, rustic-looking cabins were shown in a third picture. She read aloud the snippets of text. " 'Tired of offices, computers, traffic, and all the other trials of life? Would you like to live free of these burdens? Does getting away from disagreeable, disgruntled people sound good to you? Then come and enjoy true harmony with our family at Wisdom's Design.' "

"Believe me, it's as wonderful as it sounds. Wisdom — she's our leader — allows each of us to be who we were meant to be." Freedom exhaled a contented sigh.

"So you make your living selling what you make at the commune?"

He bristled. "We don't use the term 'commune.' The world has sullied that word so it has negative energy. And anyway," Freedom continued, "I've already contributed my trust fund to Wisdom's Design."

"Your trust fund?" Joelle could only imagine Freedom's background and how heartbroken his parents must have been to see their son taken in by a cult leader.

He shrugged. "I don't need the money. I'd rather spend my time making other seekers aware of Wisdom's Design than working myself into the cardiac unit at the hospital like my father did." Anger clouded his features.

"I'm sorry."

"Don't be. He created his own destiny." Freedom pasted on a smile. "Now why don't you create yours by helping me hand out these brochures? We only have five hundred. It shouldn't take long to distribute them."

"You're here to hand out materials about your co — whatever it is?"

"And to meet you, of course."

"Even if I were willing, this mall doesn't attract that many people. Getting rid of that many pamphlets will take all night," she protested. "Besides, when you suggested we meet here, I thought maybe you had plans for a movie. The Silver Screen Matinee is in progress, you know."

"Silver Screen Matinee?" His look was blank. "No, I had no plans to go to a movie. I don't care to see what the world has to offer." Freedom's look changed to one of genuine puzzlement. "I can't believe you're suggesting we waste time in a theater. You seem so spiritual. I thought you agreed with me."

"I do agree that some of the things the world offers aren't good, but they're not all bad, either." She remembered something Dean told her once. "As Christians, we are to be in the world, but not of it."

He held up a leaflet and tapped it with his forefinger. "That describes Wisdom's Design exactly."

Joelle found herself praying to the Holy Spirit. She needed to be shown what words to say. Within a split second, she answered. "Not exactly. Wisdom is not a person, but God the Father. The only way we can find God the Father is through the Lord, His Son, Jesus Christ."

Freedom shook his head. "There are many paths to God."

"Not according to the Bible. Jesus said He is the way, the truth, and the life. No one comes to God the Father except by Him."

"I disagree. That viewpoint is too narrow for my mind."

Joelle rose from her metal seat. "I'm sorry, Freedom, but I just don't think this is working. If you change your mind and want to learn more about the Lord — the true Savior — you can call me. I work for Dr.

Mulligan. You can reach me there every weekday."

Joelle saw Freedom open his mouth to protest, but she turned before he could make his next point. Bailing out on an evening wasn't easy for Joelle. She had been brought up to be polite, even to the point of putting up with boredom, inconvenience, and expense, but she could see talking further to Freedom was useless. He was lost, and she wasn't about to hand out materials urging others to take the wrong path. She sent up a silent petition that Freedom would one day come to Christ. In the meantime, she prayed that she had planted a seed.

Discouraged, she was in no mood to shop and certainly in no frame of mind to sit alone in a theater. She decided to leave the mall, go home, microwave a bag of popcorn, and watch one of her dad's old movies on the VCR. Maybe becoming engrossed in a story with a happy ending was the answer.

Joelle was just about to step onto the crosswalk when she spotted a brunette with a fussy hairdo and an auburn-haired male form she instantly recognized. Disinclined to being caught on her way back from a bombed evening, Joelle looked at her black flats.

"Joelle!"

Too late. Dean had already seen her.

CHAPTER 19

Nicole nudged Dean, sending a sharp pain through his ribs. "Do you have to speak to Joelle? She didn't see us," she hissed.

"Of course I want to speak to Joelle. She's my best friend." Dean didn't add that he'd been thinking about Joelle all evening. In fact, he'd been thinking about Joelle often as the weeks passed. He'd spent considerable time at the retreat praying about whether or not the Lord wanted him to pursue a romantic relationship with her. The more time passed, the more Dean became convinced it was the right thing to do. Otherwise, why would he feel such a sense of peace after praying about her, and why else would Joelle continue to weigh on his mind?

In the meantime, Dean wasn't surprised by Nicole's objection. He'd made a huge mistake in asking Nicole to see *The Sound of Music* with him after his attempts to reach

Joelle failed. Ever since, Nicole had clung to him like static electricity. He'd never seen such a chameleon in action.

After their first disastrous night together, Dean never expected to hear from Nicole again. To his surprise, she later begged his forgiveness. When he accepted her apology on the condition she cool off, she molted into a student in search of a spiritual mentor. Over the past weeks, she'd seemed eager to learn more about the Lord. So when she invited him to the Silver Screen Matinee, Dean saw no reason not to tag along.

This night had turned out no differently from the first. Over dinner, he realized Nicole's spiritual quest was a ruse to launch a hoped-for romance. The proverbial last straw broke when Dean handed her a list of suggested religious books.

"What is it with you and religion?" Nicole asked over veal parmesan. Her voice revealed her disgust. "Don't you ever talk about anything else?"

Dean's surprise was genuine. "I thought you wanted a book list. You asked me what you could read in addition to scripture."

"Of course I want to read, but I can't stay focused on religion every minute of the day. There are other things in life, you know. Things like —" she drummed her fingers on the table, "fun."

"Fun? But I have lots of fun," he protested.

"I mean real fun." Fork midway in the air, she leaned toward him, her voice becoming husky. "You seem to forget I'm a woman and you're a man."

His consciousness returning to the present, Dean shuddered. He wasn't fond of hurting people, especially when they were as wobbly in their spiritual walk as Nicole, but he could see she wasn't going to give up on a romantic relationship. That was something he couldn't offer her. Better to hurt Nicole now than to give her false hope.

Dean made a deal with himself. He would keep his promise to watch the movie with her. Then he would make sure he was never alone with Nicole again. Ever.

Thankfully, Joelle was only steps away, but she seemed to be concentrating on the pavement. As soon as they reached her at the end of the crosswalk, he said, "Find any loose change?"

Joelle stopped and looked up. "Not yet, but I'm feeling lucky." Her flat voice and sour expression told another tale.

"If I believed in luck, I'd say you are fortunate," Dean said.

"I do believe in chance. So keep looking,"

Nicole advised, "and maybe your luck will pay off."

Dean hoped Joelle would ignore Nicole's snide remark. "We're lucky because we ran into you. Unless you're in too much of a hurry to talk."

"I'll bet she is." Nicole looked at her with a steady gaze. "I'm sure Joelle is on her way to somewhere important."

"Not really," Joelle answered, shaking her head. "I was just on my way home."

Dean couldn't resist seizing the opportunity. "Then why don't you join Nicole and me? We're on our way to the Silver Screen Matinee. They're featuring Jimmy Stewart movies. 'It's a Wonderful Life' starts at seven forty-five."

"And it's almost that time now." Nicole tugged on Dean's arm. "We'd better hurry, Dean. I'd hate to miss the beginning."

"I think that's the only Christmas movie I don't mind seeing in June." Joelle smiled warmly until her gaze shot to Nicole. Dean could feel her stewing in fury. Apparently, Joelle could sense her anger, too. "But I think I'll take a pass this time. I don't want to impose on your evening."

Nicole let out a breath. "Some other time, then —"

"Nonsense, Joelle. You won't be imposing," Dean rushed to argue. "We'd love to have you join us."

Joelle's lips tightened as though she were uncertain, but he could tell even underneath her teal contacts that her eyes were sparkling. "I don't know —"

Dean interlocked his elbow with Nicole's, then stepped forward and did the same with Joelle. "Aw, have pity on a guy. How often do I have the chance to escort a beautiful blond and a gorgeous brunette to a movie at the same time?"

To his relief, both women tittered at his compliments. Dean smiled to himself. Already he was keeping his resolution not to be alone with Nicole.

In the theater, Joelle sat on one side of Dean, and Nicole sat on the other. Joelle tried to ignore Nicole's obvious flirtations. She watched as Dean remained polite but indifferent. She had a feeling her presence wasn't holding him back from responding with enthusiasm to his date. Joelle couldn't help but shake her head. If Nicole had any perception about Dean's personality, she would know he'd never react well to such blatant ploys, at least not for long.

But who was she to criticize Nicole? Joelle hadn't been thinking about the movie as they sat together. All she could contemplate were the events of the past months. Why hadn't she seen the obvious? Why hadn't she considered Sir Dean as her knight in shining armor all along, instead of foolishly chasing a dream? He was already her best friend. He knew her better than anyone else did. What better basis for a lasting love?

At that moment, Nicole placed a bold hand on Dean's. She whispered something in his ear, causing them both to giggle. Despite her brave thoughts from before, Joelle's heart betrayed her confidence with a fearful lurch. What if she was already too late? Unbidden tears filled her eyes. Joelle placed her fingers on the inside corner of each eye, hoping she could pass off her upset as seasonal allergy symptoms. But as they began to fall in earnest, she realized that excuse would never work. She sniffled.

Dean's arm wrapped around her in response. He whispered in her ear, "Happy endings always did make you cry."

A nod of the head was all the answer Joelle could muster at the moment. She wasn't so sure this ending would be a happy one.

The following Sunday after church, Joelle was surprised when Dean dropped by the house. He hadn't sat anywhere near her throughout worship or Sunday school. Even though Dean never missed Singles' Night, he had been absent the previous evening. Phone calls to his house yielded busy signals. Since he had avoided any chance to talk to her for the past two days, Joelle couldn't help but wonder if he was miffed or maybe confused. At least now she would find out.

After his assurances to Eleanor that he'd already eaten and didn't require a slice of pie or a cup of coffee, Dean followed Joelle onto the back porch. The day was mild and sunny, perfect for sitting together on the glider.

She got right to the point. "Where were you last night? I missed you at the meeting. I tried to call later to be sure you were okay, but the line was busy."

"Sorry. I — I just couldn't make it."

"Neither could Nicole." Joelle's voice was heavy with meaning. "I feel like it's my fault. I shouldn't have horned in on your date Friday night."

"It's not your fault. If anyone needs to be blamed, it's me." He placed his hand on hers. "I told Nicole when I took her home that I couldn't see her again outside of church."

Emotions — a mixture of triumph, happiness, and wonder — churned through her. "But I thought she liked you" was all she could manage.

He looked at his athletic shoes. "I think she did, but the feeling just wasn't mutual."

After witnessing Dean's lack of enthusiasm toward Nicole at the movie theater, she couldn't say she was surprised. Curious, but not surprised. "So what happened between you two?"

He shook his head. "Nothing major, but it's nothing I want to discuss."

"Oh." Tight-lipped, Dean was obviously not going to reveal more. She decided the best course was for her to respect his wishes to remain silent, and to confess her own feelings. "About those guys I met through the personal ads —"

Turning his face toward Joelle, Dean held up his palm as a signal for her to stop talking. "You don't have to explain anything to me." He placed his hand back in his lap, a distressed look shadowing his boyish face. "Unless you need to tell me you've found someone you're planning to see a lot more of."

"No." Shaking her head rapidly to emphasize her point, Joelle let out a sigh. "I guess you're right. It's probably better if we don't share each other's misery. At least not about other dates. Especially since I've come to realize . . ." She couldn't finish, choosing instead to stare at her sandaled feet.

"Come to realize what?"

Joelle looked up and saw his hazel eyes opening wide. She swallowed and returned her gaze to her feet. "That no one compares to you," she said softly. She waited for his response, conscious all the while of her beating heart.

"I could have told you that."

She looked into his face. Discovering a broad grin was no surprise. "Oh, you!" She tapped him playfully on the shoulder. Unwilling to let go of the opportunity to tell him her true feelings, Joelle turned serious. "From the moment I met the first guy, I found myself comparing him to you. It was the same with the others. They always came up short." She smiled. "But it was really at the theater on Friday night that everything came together."

"That night, huh?" Dean looked back at her, gazing into her eyes.

Suddenly she knew she could look into those eyes forever. She became engrossed in his face, the straight nose, the fine features that had become so familiar. Joelle found herself looking at his lips, wondering if he might —

"Joelle, I don't think we should see each other again."

She bolted up in her seat, her torso moving away from him. Her eyes widened so much that her lashes seemed to touch the skin underneath her eyebrow. "Say what?"

Joelle hoped she'd misunderstood. Surely she hadn't just spilled out her feelings, only to be rejected! She folded her arms over her chest, each hand clutching the opposite elbow. The motion, she knew, was a subconscious attempt to protect herself. Only it was too late. She'd made herself vulnerable.

Fool!

Her voice shook as she uttered the next question. "What do you mean?"

"Let me finish." His voice dropped to a whisper. "I don't think we should see each other until your mom's surprise party."

Her fingers tightened their grip. His words were of some comfort, but it felt like a hollow victory. "But that's two whole weeks from now. What about our rehearsals? We're supposed to sing our duet soon, aren't we?" Her voice was shrill.

He pressed his finger to his rounded lips. "Shh! I know. I already called and arranged to have it postponed until next month. Mandy's been wanting to sing her solo, anyway."

Joelle remained silent.

"What's the matter?" He smiled a boyish smile. "Don't think you can do without me that long?"

She didn't know whether to laugh or strangle Dean for his attempt at humor. She resisted both urges. Dean's usual way of coping with unexpected emotions was to employ wit. Best to respond in kind. Deliberately she arched an eyebrow. "I didn't think you could do without me for that long."

"Maybe I can't." His smile turned bittersweet. "But I think this will be good for us — not easy for me, but good for us." Gently, he took her hands from her elbows and guided them into his. Her small hands protected in his larger ones, Joelle felt as though her entire being was secure. "While I was at the retreat, I invested a lot of prayer time in us," Dean told her. "I think I know what the Lord wants us to do. But now I want to give you time to confer with Him. I'll keep praying, too." The longing in his eyes was unmistakable. "If I pray when you're anywhere in the vicinity, I won't be able to hear God."

Though the enormity of his words didn't escape her, Joelle couldn't help but protest. "But can't we just follow our feelings? I mean, you must be thinking the same thing I am — that we were meant to be together."

"True." He nodded once more. "But I don't want to pursue a deeper relationship with you based entirely on feelings. Emotions are fickle and can't always be trusted. If I'd gone with my feelings, I'd have made a major play for you a long time ago." His mouth curved into a sheepish grin.

"Really?" Joelle wondered. Dean had always been the gentleman, never even hinting he'd like to be more than friends.

"Really. I know I've hidden my feelings well all this time."

"Why?" she asked. "What stopped you from telling me how you feel?"

"The day you accepted the altar call, it was like a part of me was there with you. I thought it would be unfair to make my feelings about you known then. You were at a high point in your life, having accepted Christ, really and truly accepted His saving grace. You didn't need those complications."

"Says who? If you'd let me decide that for myself, you'd have saved me the trouble of going through a lot of bad dates," she pointed out only half-jokingly.

"Maybe so, but have you considered that it could have been the Lord's plan for you to meet those other guys? Now if He wants us to be together, you could really appreciate me." Dean flashed her a charming smile, letting her know his observation wasn't motivated by bloated ego. "And maybe I needed to spend some time with Nicole as part of the process of confirming my feelings."

"Makes sense," she agreed. "But since we've both gone through this process, we should be all set."

"Not yet. Not until we both know the Lord's answer for certain." Breaking his earnest expression, Dean grinned. "Besides, if I'm going to ruin a perfectly good friendship, I want to be sure I'm exchanging it for something even better."

Two weeks later, Joelle was nervous as she and her mother walked up to the front porch of the Jamison home. Joelle was grateful her dad had chosen her to provide distraction so her mom wouldn't be tipped off about the surprise party. Joelle was so excited that the thought of preparing to greet a houseful of party guests was more than she could handle. She was glad her visiting sisters-in-law were up for the job.

Dean had made himself scarce for fourteen days. As he asked, she'd been in prayer about their relationship. Each time she prayed, she was assured that her feelings about Dean were right. She thanked the Lord for the ability to acknowledge them. Then, selfishly, she prayed Dean would decide to court her. Today she would know if her prayers, both selfish and unselfish, would be answered.

In the meantime, she couldn't wait to see the look on her mom's face when she saw that all four of her sons and their families had come to the celebration — two only a few minutes by car, and two by plane. They could all be thankful Mom had given up her last year of high school to marry and start her family. For the first time in her young life, Joelle understood how her mom could feel a love so powerful that she gave up her education.

"That was fun, Joelle," Mom said as she stepped onto the porch. "We should go out for coffee more often."

"I'd like that," Joelle answered loudly enough for those inside to hear. She didn't want to take a chance the partygoers inside would miss her mom's entrance.

"Good. I don't need a hearing aid, you know." The older woman chuckled as she unlocked the front door. She stepped into the living room.

A chorus of voices rang out. "SUR-

PRISE!"

"Surpize, Gam!" two-year-old Todd added belatedly.

Good-humored laughter flooded the house. Todd clapped his hands, congratulating himself that his greeting had been so well received.

Eleanor was speechless. The look of amazement mixed with pleasure on her mother's face was one Joelle would never forget. Flashes from several cameras blinked brightly as Eleanor gawked at the room full of family and friends, surrounded by lots of streamers and balloons. Dad had even made a banner on the computer. It read "Congratulations to Our Graduate."

Dad stepped forward and gave his wife a big bear hug. "Congratulations, honey. After all these years, you did it!"

She nodded, and tears suddenly began to flow down her cheeks. The crowd murmured their approval and broke out into applause. Joelle knew this was one of the happiest days of her mother's life.

After she gave her mother a hug and endured a loving lecture about her part in the charade, Joelle turned and faced Dean. Eyes alight, he nodded to her before greeting the guest of honor. Joelle felt her own face brighten upon seeing him again. She wished she could take his hand and get away from everyone at that moment, but etiquette demanded otherwise. Joelle wished Dean hadn't chosen the day of the party to see her again. Disinclined to look too eager, Joelle made the rounds among the other guests and caught up with her four brothers and gave their wives and their children a round of hugs before she allowed herself anywhere near Dean.

As the party progressed, Joelle kept looking for an opening so she and Dean could talk. Over and over, she could see no hope for any privacy. Giving up, she decided to wait until the party wound down and only her family remained. Since she was occupied by the duties expected of her as daughter of the house, Joelle managed to keep her mind off her nervousness as the hours passed. She could only hope Dean's prayers had confirmed his earlier feelings.

By the time the party was over, night had fallen. Joelle was in the kitchen, putting up the last bit of leftover cake, when she felt a warm hand on her shoulder. "Did you miss me?" Dean's whispered voice flowed into her ear.

His warm breath sent a shiver down her spine. "Why don't you come with me and find out?" She sealed the cake box, then led him outdoors to the empty floral-patterned glider on the back porch. Her heart was beating rapidly as Dean sat close beside her.

"Don't tell your mom this, but I didn't think the party would ever end."

"Me, either." She giggled. "Your secret's safe with me."

"I hope so. You've been avoiding me all day."

"I wouldn't have if I thought there was a shred of hope we could have some privacy. I couldn't run away from the party."

"You've got a point." He took her hands in his. He held them firmly but not too tightly. "So did you pray?"

"Yes. I prayed every day. How about you?"

"The same. And I got the same answer. I know this is what the Lord wants for my life, and the time is right." He looked deeply into her eyes. "But if you got a different answer, I'll wait."

"No, I'm certain. I don't want to wait."

"Neither do I." Leaning closer, he wrapped her in his embrace. When his lips touched hers, she knew she was where she belonged.

EPILOGUE

Months later

Joelle and her father watched as her sister-in-law, Susan, as matron of honor, walked down the aisle. Her rust-colored chiffon dress looked good with her flowing blond hair. Autumn flowers filled the sanctuary of the small country church.

Joelle had awakened that morning to blue skies that suggested a summer day, yet brisk mountain air revealed that October had arrived.

Joelle remembered returning from her hair appointment around lunchtime. The familiar smell of her neighbor burning leaves filled the air. Happily, she hummed a few lines of "Beauty for Ashes." Ever since she and Dean sang the song together in church, everyone they knew associated the tune with them.

The bride searched the side of the altar and spotted auburn-haired Mandy. She had sung the song beautifully as part of the ceremony. Joelle resisted the urge to hum it once more.

Aware that in just a moment all eyes would be upon her, Joelle self-consciously smoothed her dress by extending the fingers of the hand that held her tiny white Bible. In the other hand, she held a bouquet of white roses that complemented her lace-covered white silk gown. Joelle had chosen long sleeves with a mandarin-style collar, a full, flowing skirt, and modest train. Her veil was simple and added no height.

"You've never looked more beautiful, Joelle," Dad said.

She looked into his eyes. "I've never felt more beautiful." Joelle meant it. Over the past months, she had grown in her relationships — with Dean, with the friends they shared, and with their families. Most importantly, the time had given them a chance to grow together in their faith. For the first time in her life, Joelle felt worthy to walk down the church aisle to meet her groom. Once joined, together they would walk side by side in love, in faith, in life.

The wait had been long but well worth every minute.

She took the last seconds before Susan took her place beside the other bridesmaids to say a silent prayer. *Lord, please walk with Dean and me as we marry today, and for the rest of our lives. We pray that, as we marry in Your will, we will please You in every aspect of our marriage. In Your Son Jesus' name, amen.*

Her stomach leapt with anticipation at the first strains of the "Bridal March." On cue, all two hundred wedding guests stood, turning their heads to see her veiled form. Dean waited at the altar, a look of anticipation covering his face. The elusive Mr. Perfect was no longer out of reach. After this day, he would be hers.

Forever.

The employees of Thorndike Press hope you have enjoyed this Large Print book. All our Thorndike and Wheeler Large Print titles are designed for easy reading, and all our books are made to last. Other Thorndike Press Large Print books are available at your library, through selected bookstores, or directly from us.

For information about titles, please call:
(800) 223-1244

or visit our Web site at:
www.gale.com/thorndike
www.gale.com/wheeler

To share your comments, please write:
Publisher
Thorndike Press
295 Kennedy Memorial Drive
Waterville, ME 04901